LAL
BOOK ONE

*To Denise~
Thanks so much
for your help
+ support!*

Tracey Cramer-Kelly

Take Two

A Hollywood Romance

Tracey CRAMER-KELLY

LADY BIKER SERIES
BOOK ONE

Take Two A Hollywood Romance

Copyright © 2013 Tracey Cramer-Kelly
Published by Twiggle T Productions
St. Francis, Minnesota 55070

ISBN: 1-4921-7312-6
EAN-13: 97-81492-17312-0

Printed in the United States of America

foreword

As a biker chick myself for 20+ years, I dedicate this series to all the women riders I know. To those who wondered why I hadn't yet written about bikers… this one's for you!

For the curious: In *Take Two*, the characters are filming a movie about a wounded military veteran with PTSD. That "movie" is actually my book, *True Surrender*.

chapter 1

Zac Davies peered at his co-star through a haze of dancing spots that reminded him of times as a kid when his parents' old TV went to static. He still managed his lines, but they were flat, even to his own ears. He took a step toward Lydia and stumbled.

"Cut!" The director called.

Damn it.

Zac ducked his head, raking his hand through his hair. The Vicodin had held the headache at bay—so far—but these dizzy spells were another matter…

He looked up in time to see Gina reach his side. "Zac, I want to see you in my trailer," she said in her usual no-nonsense demeanor. "Everyone else, take five."

Great.

Being summoned to the director's trailer was like being sent to the principal's office. Yet in the three-plus weeks they'd been shooting, Gina Devereaux had shown herself true to her reputation: tough but fair. Not to mention damn good at what she did; with her guidance, he'd done some of his best work yet.

This is what it's like in the big leagues.

At twenty-nine, the golden window of opportunity was closing fast. This was his big break. He couldn't afford to blow it. He owed it to his parents.

He felt sweat trickle down his back.

"Take a seat, Zac." Gina pointed to a cot set up to the side of the trailer. She went straight to a cooler at the back and pulled out two water bottles. She handed one to Zac and he opened it gratefully.

She pulled a chair and sat so that she faced him.

"Are you okay?"

It was not what he'd expected to hear, and he hesitated. Should he tell her? "Um...the heat has been getting to me," he said. "Maybe I'm just dehydrated."

Her eyes narrowed and he braced himself for anger or frustration.

"You've been really solid up until the last couple days," she said. "Have you been partying with the crew at night? Drinking a lot of alcohol?"

"No."

"Taking drugs?"

"Of course not!" Zac said. "I don't do drugs."

"Well, then, what's your explanation?" Irritation was creeping into her voice. She was under as much pressure as he was. Maybe more. "Because you don't go from giving above-the-cut performance to what I'm getting from you now."

"I know," he said. "I'm sorry. Maybe I'm just coming down with something. A flu bug. I'll take some cold medicine. I've got some in my bag."

She leaned back in her chair, studying him doubtfully.

"Gina!" The voice outside the trailer was unmistakeable.

"Shit," she muttered. "Sylvester." The film's producer was a crotchety industry veteran who had a penchant for hanging around the set and scowling at everything they did.

"I'll be out in a moment," she called.

"I'll be fine," Zac said, even as the beginning of what promised to become another ferocious headache snaked across his temples.

I have to get to the Vicodin before this turns into stomach cramps.

"I think you need to rest," she said, still watching him in an unnerving way.

"Just let me get my bag…"

She stood. "You stay here. Lay down and close your eyes for a few minutes. I'll send someone with your bag."

It was only a matter of minutes before a production assistant showed up with his bag. Zac rummaged at the bottom, found the Vicodin and popped two of them.

Does Vicodin count as a drug? Nah. Not the kind of drugs she was asking about…

He tried to relax but he was overly warm even here with the rudimentary air conditioning. He ran a hand across his forehead; it was sweaty too.

When Gina came back, she looked none too happy. "I've been overruled," she said. "I need you back on the set in five."

He nodded.

"I'll send Suzie in here to touch up your makeup."

*　　*　　*　　*　　*　　*　　*　　*　　*　　*　　*　　*　　*

Gina stood behind Camera Two, squinting at the actors. She had serious doubts they'd get any usable footage this day, and it was becoming harder to keep her frustration in check. She *needed* this film to be successful. But if they didn't get it this time, she was calling it a day regardless of Sylvester's opinion. "Action!" she called for the fifth time.

Had she been wrong about Zac's ability? Wrong in thinking that she'd be able to bring out the best in him? Maybe those first weeks were just too good to be true?

She watched him closely. She may have been the only one to notice the slight slur on his first lines. Then he sharpened. He took his co-star, Lydia Grant, by the hand as he spun off his lines.

Damn, we just might get this.

Lydia took over with her lines as they moved between the trees as scripted. The cameras followed, and so did Gina.

The script called for Lydia to stumble and Zac to catch her, but it didn't go as planned.

Instead, Zac got dragged down *with* Lydia.

Gina didn't call a stop to the action; rather, she waited to see what they would do. She knew her camera people would follow her lead, and so would the actors. If it wasn't good, they wouldn't use it; that's what post-production was for. But experience had taught her that every now and then, while deep in character, the camera could catch something in the actors' performance that just…*worked*. Better than the script.

Zac stayed down as Lydia got to her knees. She produced a demure chuckle and offered him her hand. Gina was focused on the small movements of the hand, the face, the eye as Zac got to his feet. So she was probably the first to notice Zac's face go pale.

Then, as if in slow motion, his eyes rolled back into his head and his body crumpled to the ground.

Oh no!

For a moment there was silence, as if everyone was waiting to see what the actors would do. But Zac didn't move, and Lydia's face held a stunned look.

"Cut!" Gina rushed forward and dropped to her knees. "Zac!"

Lydia was beside her on her knees now too. "Did he hit his head?"

Gina placed one hand behind Zac's neck. "Zac, can you hear me?" She heard Dale, her assistant director and close friend, on the radio requesting the set medic.

She placed her other hand flat against Zac's chest. To her relief, his breathing was regular and his heartbeat strong. She brought her hand up to his forehead; she couldn't tell if he was running a fever or just overly warm from the sun and exertion. "Zac, if you can hear me, I need you to open your eyes."

No response.

"Oh man…" Lydia sounded freaked out. She took one of Zac's hands in her own.

Now Dale was asking the camera operators to review the footage they'd just shot. It was a good idea; perhaps one of the camera angles would show if he'd hit his head.

The medic knelt next to Gina. "What happened?" she said.

"I think he fainted," Gina said. "But he may have also hit his head."

The medic performed an assessment, taking extra time to feel around on Zac's head. She flashed a small light in his eyes. "Pupils look good," she said. "No head trauma."

"He was obviously out last night partying too hard." Sylvester's voice cut over the murmurs of the crew. When Gina looked up she was surprised to find that the producer stood less than ten feet away.

"I don't know about that," Gina said. Of course, Sylvester didn't know what Zac had told her. "I think we should have him checked out."

"Gina, he *fainted*." Sylvester glared at her. "A hospital visit would bring the tabloids on us like flies on shit."

"Then bring a doctor in to look at him," she said.

"The medic can keep an eye on him, and you can work on a scene that doesn't require him," Sylvester said.

Gina looked at the medic; she just shrugged.

Sylvester narrowed his eyes at the cast and crew. "And not a word of this to anyone outside the set."

"No." Gina stood, hands on her hips. "I let you push *me* into pushing *him*. If you want him looked after here, I'm going to personally make sure he's all right." She addressed the crew and cast in a firm voice: "That's a wrap for today, folks."

She turned to Dale and the medic. "Can you help get him to my trailer?"

Dale nodded and motioned to one of the production assistants.

"Gina—" Sylvester started.

"Damn it, Syl," She cut him off with a murderous glare. "*Get off my set.*"

chapter 2

Zac was dimly aware of a wet pressure on his forehead.

"Zachariah."

His full name...Aunt Trudy?

He inhaled a careful breath, licked his lips, swallowed.

"He's coming around." The same voice. Not Aunt Trudy.

"How long has he been out?" Another voice. Male this time. The squeak of a chair hinge.

"About fifteen minutes, I think." The wet pressure retreated.

"Still running a fever?"

A lighter touch on his forehead. "Still."

He opened his eyes and tried to make sense of the woman who perched on the edge of the cot next to him.

Holy shit!

His left hand pressed against the cot in an attempt to raise himself.

"Take it easy, Zac." Gina's hand went to his other wrist, which lay across his abdomen. He let himself fall back as a sudden pain sliced into his temples.

His eyes left Gina and wandered the trailer—yes, he was in the director's trailer—then went to Dale (who stood next to the chair) and back to Gina. *This doesn't look good.* "What happened?"

"You fainted in the middle of the scene," Gina said.

He groaned and ran a hand behind his head. That meant the entire crew had seen it. *And Sylvester...*

"Do you want me to get the medic?" Dale asked.

"No," Gina said. "I want to hear from Zac first. How do you feel?"

It felt like a woodpecker had taken up residence inside his skull. "I have a raging headache," he muttered. "I need Vicodin."

"Vicodin?" Gina said.

Damn. What was he thinking, saying that out loud? But it was hard to think clearly...

"Nothing else was working." He rubbed his temples. "It was from a back injury I had last year."

"Zac, you should have told me you were feeling that badly."

"I didn't think that was a good idea," he said. "Not given our conversation..."

Gina's face took on a stricken look.

"Besides," he continued. "I thought it was just the flu."

A wave of nausea washed over him. *Oh, no.* This could *not* be happening...

He moaned softly. "Not again!" He waved toward the small garbage basket that sat by the chair.

Gina swiped up the basket and handed it to him just in time. He leaned away from her as his stomach twisted in on itself and he heaved into the basket.

"Sorry," he rasped when he could catch his breath. "This headache makes me nauseous."

He was surprised to find she hadn't left her perch next to him.

Her face was a mask of concern as she asked, "What do you mean by 'not again'?"

She noticed Zac's hesitation. "No acting, Zac. Please. Just the straight-up truth."

He sighed; he hadn't the energy for this. "I woke last night with terrible stomach cramps. I threw up a couple times."

"That's it." She stood and moved toward the desk. "We're taking you to the hospital."

"Ourselves?" Dale said. "No medic transport?"

"In my car." She tossed him the keys. "You drive."

"Sylvester won't like it," Dale said.

"Screw him," Gina said. "We should have taken him when this first happened. You know how to get there?"

"Affirmative."

"Bring the car as close to the trailer as you can. If we're quiet about it maybe I won't have to deal with Syl until after we find out what's wrong."

Gina picked up Zac's backpack and slid it onto her shoulders. Then she slipped her own purse over her head so that it hung across her chest.

"You really don't have to go to all this trouble." Zac struggled to a sitting position, eyeing his backpack. "I'm sure if I got a couple days rest…"

"Come on." Gina sat down next to him. "I'll help you. Just go slow."

Zac put his feet on the ground and his hands in Gina's. Slowly he got to his feet. He stood there, swaying slightly as the room swirled around him.

Gina's arm came around his waist. "I'm not strong enough to catch you if you fall," she said. "So you've got to let me help you."

He let his arm come down around her shoulder somewhat timidly.

"Better," she said. "Now I think we'll make it."

*   *   *   *   *   *   *   *   *   *   *   *   *

The moment the car started moving, Zac was sick again. And he didn't stop. Couldn't stop. And damn it all, he was spread across his *boss's lap* with a bucket in his face.

You're a real professional, Davies.

And then it was difficult to care *where* he was; as dry heaves wracked his body and blackness buzzed at the edges of his vision, he could only pray that the hospital was close and the movement would stop.

I am in hell.

And then, somehow, he was on a gurney in a hospital room, still curled up and clutching the bucket. Gina's voice floated somewhere overhead. He tried to concentrate on the doctor's words: *Food poisoning. Stomach pumped.* The prick of a needle in his arm. "Sedative…relax…"

And now this doctor's face hovered over his, saying "relax, Zac, relax."

Who was he kidding? He wasn't the one with a tube being shoved down his throat!

I am in hell.

chapter 3

Gina paced the hallway outside Zac's room. She knew Sylvester was on his way because Gerri had told her so. That was a bad sign; normally he just called and yelled over the phone. Dale had made himself scarce as soon as he'd heard. But Gina couldn't take a chance she'd miss him; she didn't want him to reach Zac in the shape he was in.

Gerri, Sylvester's personal assistant, would take care of the hospital details and get in touch with Zac's agent and family. But for now, apparently, Zac's care was Gina's responsibility.

Even though she was watching for him and mentally preparing for it, Gina was still startled when she heard Sylvester's angry voice at the nurse's station. "Where the hell is my actor?"

She strode toward him. "Syl."

"What the hell, Gina?" He turned his piercing gaze on her. "You drag my actor off the set without alerting me?"

"There was no time," she said. "He's very sick."

"He *passed out*," Sylvester said. "What, too much partying last night? The kid's got a lot of nerve…"

"It's not like that," she said. "The doctor thinks he's got food poisoning."

"I want him back on the set tomorrow."

It was as if the man hadn't even heard what she said! She'd worked with Sylvester a long time but...damn, this was just too much. "This is a human being we're talking about, Syl," Gina said sternly. "Not a robot or a part you can simply replace."

"I *should* replace him," Sylvester said. "These actors get a big head, think the film is all about them."

Gina lost her grip on civility. "If you want to fire Zac, then you might as well fire me, too. Because I don't want to work for someone who places more importance on a *film* than on the people who make it happen."

That shut him up, but only momentarily. "There's a lot of money riding on this being pulled off on schedule."

"So you're saying the *money* is also more important than Zac's life." Gina crossed her arms.

"You're getting dramatic," he said. "The kid is sick, not dying. I'm just saying..."

"I know what you're saying," she said disgustedly. "Who do you think slaved over the schedule? We've shot almost half the footage. If you fire him now, I'll quit too. You'll have to find a new director *and* a new leading man and re-shoot it all. Then your schedule truly *will* be screwed."

He opened his mouth in astonishment, but she cut him off. "But just as important, the work Zac's done up to now has been damn good. And you know it."

She stared at him until he was forced to respond. "Yeah, the kid's done some good stuff," he muttered.

"Send everyone home for the weekend," she said. "By then we'll have a better idea when Zac can come back. Hell, it might not even be long for all we know."

"It better not be," Syl growled. But he was already backing up, looking about the hospital with obvious distaste. "Well, then..."

"I'll take care of the details here," she said. "You put the word out at the set."

"Fine," he said. "I'll tell them as little as possible. Make sure this is kept quiet. The *last* thing we need is tabloid rumors."

Gina waited until he'd left, then let out her breath. *Slowly, count to ten…*

She jumped when she heard the doctor's voice behind her. "Miss Devereaux?"

How much had he heard? She pasted a neutral look on her face before turning toward him.

"I'm Mister Davies' specialist, Thomas Carrini. I'm a nephrologist, and I specialize in diseases related to the kidneys."

Gina took his hand. He was only an inch taller than her and probably the same age, but she noticed right away that his eyes were kind.

"I need to talk to you about Zac," he said.

"Can it wait?" she said. "We should be able to reach his family soon."

"I don't think so," the doctor said. "Nothing turned up in Zac's stomach contents. At least, nothing we could identify that would make him sick. We need to run blood tests to check his liver function."

"Is that serious?"

"It depends on what we find," he said.

*   *   *   *   *   *   *   *   *   *   *   *   *

Gina ran a hand over her face, suddenly feeling every one of her forty-one years. How in the world did she get caught up in this? She shook her head, then brushed past the curtain in Zac's room.

He lay still, his breathing steady and even. She was surprised how relieved she felt, knowing he was safe and under care here in the hospital. It had been awful in the car; she'd felt so helpless... and guilty. Had she really thought he'd been doing drugs?

She didn't know he was awake until he spoke. "I heard you and Sylvester arguing."

"Don't worry about him right now." She lowered herself into the chair beside his bed.

"But you could lose your job." His eyes sought hers, and she didn't look away.

"I don't think he'll fire me." She still couldn't believe she'd given Sylvester that ultimatum; she needed this job. How many times had she told her daughters there would be times in their lives they'd have to stand up for what was right even when they stood to lose something?

"Sylvester is arrogant and abrasive, but he isn't stupid," she said.

"But he'll let me go." Zac looked away. "And this was supposed to be my big break."

"Don't go there, Zac," she said. "This is a temporary setback only. Nobody's getting fired."

Zac didn't respond.

"For now, I've convinced him to suspend production for a few days," Gina said. "We'll figure out what's making you sick and you'll be on the mend."

She placed her hand on his arm. "Okay?"

Zac gave her a weak smile. "If you say so, Director."

chapter 4

Gina had barely closed her hotel room door when there was a knock on it. She opened it to find one of the production crew.

"Miss Devereaux." The girl fidgeted, wringing her hands. "I'm sorry to bother you, but it's really important."

Gina didn't have time for this.

"I have information about Zac and I...I don't know who else to go to," the girl said.

Gina assessed the girl. She was average in every way: mousy brown hair, glasses, nondescript clothes, worn tennis shoes. "It's Candy, isn't it?"

"Yes."

In Gina's experience, the quieter the crew member was, the more they knew everyone's business. They didn't talk much; they *watched* and *listened*. It was possible Candy had information on what Zac had done outside of work the past three days. "Come in, Candy."

Candy was obviously nervous. "Miss Devereaux..."

"Call me Gina."

"Gina, I..." she said. "Zac is terribly sick, isn't he?"

"He is," Gina said.

Candy wrung her hands. "I should have told someone."

Gina took the girl's hands and guided her to sit on the bed. "Well, I'm here now. What is it, Candy?"

"I think Sasha poisoned Zac," she blurted out.

Gina was instantly alert. "What makes you think that?"

"You know—or maybe you don't know—that Zac and Sasha were a couple?" Candy said.

Gina shook her head. She didn't follow any of that these days.

"They auditioned for this project at the same time," Candy continued. "Right after that Zac broke up with her. She was *livid*."

"Ah," Gina said. "I did pick up on some animosity between the two of them." Truthfully, she hadn't given it much thought, since they were not in any intensive scenes together.

"She's said some crummy things to him since we started shooting," Candy said. "They even had a fight. Last Friday, before the weekend break. But then, three nights ago, Sasha was in his room."

"And you know this how?"

Candy went beet red and she looked down at her hands in her lap. "I followed him."

Gina also knew this about the film industry: there was the rare stalker, but the quietly obsessed fans were much more common… and now she knew where Candy fell on this scale. "Go on."

"She brought him something—cookies or brownies," Candy said. "Like a peace offering. Only, I think the cookies were poisoned."

Gina sat back. "That's pretty far-fetched, Candy."

"I know it sounds that way," Candy said. "But think about it. That was Monday night. He started feeling badly on Tuesday. And why would she make nice to him? He dumped her. And it's not like she was going to get a better part in the film."

What should Gina make of this conversation? It was almost laughable—Sasha couldn't be that vindictive, could she? On the other hand, Gina didn't have any idea where to start, and the poison part *did* fit …

"Did you hear any of their conversation?" Gina asked.

"No," Candy admitted. "But they didn't fight, I know that much. And when she left, she didn't have the cookies with her."

Gina was silent for a spell. "Candy, I need you to do me a favor. I need you to find out if Sasha's left for the weekend."

"You believe me?"

"I have no reason to doubt what you saw," Gina said. "But it's pretty tough to believe what you're implying. I'll do this much: I will check Zac's room and see if I can find these cookies."

"You will?" Candy's gratitude was almost too much. "You can do that?"

"Meet me at Zac's room." Gina stood. "But don't let anyone see you there. And for God's sake, don't tell anyone about Zac being sick."

"That won't be a problem," Candy said. "Most of the cast doesn't even notice I'm alive."

*   *   *   *   *   *   *   *   *   *   *   *   *

Gina knocked on Dale's door. When he opened, she said, "This is going to sound crazy…"

"You know that's my specialty," he said.

"I've got to search Zac's room, but I don't want anyone to know."

As she'd hoped, Dale didn't miss a beat. "You have his pass card?"

She waved it.

"You want me to go with you?" he said.

"Actually, I want you to get the pass card for Sasha's room," she said.

Dale's eyebrows shot up. "That must be the crazy part."

"Yeah, as in desperately grasping at straws," she said. "I'll explain later. Can you do it?"

"Sure," he said. "I'll meet you at Zac's room?"

It was good to know there was at least one person on the set that she could count on no matter what. "Perfect."

*   *   *   *   *   *   *   *   *   *   *   *   *

Gina let herself into Zac's hotel room and stood blinking in the dim light. It looked like a typical bachelor pad, with clothing randomly strewn about and papers littering the small desk. She reached for the light and hesitated; was it a good idea to turn on a light?

Then she chided herself. What could she possibly hope to find if she couldn't see? She flipped the switch and headed for the desk.

It felt odd to be poking through Zac's things, especially when she wasn't exactly sure what she was looking for. The papers on the desk were almost all shooting scripts. She checked the drawers of the desk; nothing but a jumble of napkins and wet wipes.

What next? The drawers? It would really feel odd to go through his underwear…

She needed more light. She went around the bed and reached for the bedside lamp switch. The halo lit up the area, and she gawked at what she saw. "It can't be," she whispered.

There, on the nightstand, were the remains of what looked for all the world like…*oatmeal raisin cookies.*

Gina jumped at a knock on the door. Moving swiftly, she looked through the peephole and then opened the door to Candy.

"Did you find anything?" Candy said as she stepped inside.

Gina shut the door firmly behind her. "I think I found the cookies you talked about."

Candy followed Gina's gaze to the nightstand. Her eyes went wide. Gina went back to the desk. "There was a baggie in here somewhere," she muttered. "Ah, yes, here it is."

She carried the bag to the nightstand. Carefully she brushed the cookie fragments into the bag, resisting the urge to sniff at them. When she turned to Candy, she found the young woman just staring at the bag.

"I was right," Candy said softly.

"You were right about the cookies," Gina said. "Let's not jump to conclusions from there."

"I'm right," Candy said. "I know it."

"Did you find Sasha?" Gina said.

"Huh?" Candy said. "Oh. Yeah. She's in the lounge. It sounds like she's staying the night and heading out in the morning."

"What are people saying about Zac?"

"They think he's in the medic bay," Candy said. "Isn't he?"

So they'd been successful in keeping their trip to the hospital off the radar…so far.

Another knock on the door caused Candy to let out a squeak.

"That should be Dale." Gina stepped to the door and let him in. "You got the pass card?"

"That's affirmative." Dale looked from Gina to Candy, then to the bag Gina held in her hands. "But I'm getting a funny feeling about this."

Gina gave him a short explanation, then said, "I think we need to talk to Sasha."

"Maybe we should check her room first," Dale said. "That *is* why you had me get the pass card, isn't it?"

Reluctantly Gina agreed. "Candy, I think you should go hang out with whatever crew is still around tonight," Gina said. "Maybe you'll hear or see something that will help. And you can keep an eye on Sasha."

Candy looked disappointed but made no argument. At Dale's suggestion, Gina made a quick stop at her own room, where she picked up her purse and carefully stored the cookies in it. Though she felt like a criminal for the second time that night, she wasted no time in skimming through Sasha's drawers and nightstand.

"Gina," Dale said. "Take a look at this."

Gina joined him at the desk and peered at the computer printout Dale held in his hands. "It's off the internet," he said. "Some sort of poisonous mushroom…"

He lifted his eyes to Gina's. "You're not thinking—"

The text-alert on Gina's phone buzzed, startling them both. Quickly she dug the phone out of her back pocket and pressed the button for the message: *Sasha coming.*

"Shit," she said. "Let's get out of here."

Dale opened the door a crack, then closed it quickly. "Too late," he said. "She's in the hallway. Just act like you're supposed to be here."

"You've got to be kidding." Gina stuffed the papers into her purse, her mind racing. *Poisonous mushrooms?*

She took a deep, calming breath. She squared her shoulders and reminded herself of the reason she was there. *Zac is sick. Sasha might know something.*

And then Sasha was standing in the doorway. "What the hell are you doing in my room?" she demanded.

"We came to talk to you," Dale said.

"I knew these rooms weren't too secure, but seriously?" Sasha's voice rose. "You broke into my room?!"

"Look, Sasha, it's really important that we talk to you," Gina said.

Sasha eyed her warily. "About what?"

"About Zac." Gina thought she saw a flicker of wariness cross Sasha's face. "We don't want to alarm the entire crew, but... he's very sick."

"I heard he passed out at the shoot today and hit his head," Sasha said. "Heat stroke or something."

"It's a bit more involved than that," Gina said. "He passed out because he was already sick. No one knew how sick he'd been because he covered it well. Dizziness, stomach cramps, vomiting, fever... After that incident, it got so bad we had to take him to the hospital. The doctor seems to think that Zac ingested some sort of poison."

"So now you're accusing me of poisoning him?" Sasha said. "Oh, this is rich. This is just too much."

"I'm not accusing anyone of anything," Gina said. "I'm simply checking out any and every possibility. Because we really need to find out what kind of toxin is in his system."

Sasha stood with her arms crossed angrily, glaring at Gina. It took all of Gina's willpower to keep her voice even. "I understand that you dated for awhile and I thought you might still be close to him."

"No," Sasha said. "We're not close. Just acquaintances. That's all."

"So you haven't spent any time with him lately? Just the two of you?"

"Of course not."

Gina glanced at Dale, then turned her attention back to Sasha. "You didn't visit him in his room the other night?"

Sasha's face flushed but she said nothing.

Gina held her tongue—and the younger woman's gaze.

Finally Sasha blew out a breath. "He's just like every other man," she said. "Taking what he wants and giving nothing in return. Full of himself, never interested in what I need. Only in his precious *career*. And when he'd gotten what he wanted from me, he tossed me aside like I was nothing."

Gina's cell phone chirped, and she glanced at the display.

"He doesn't deserve to be famous. He doesn't deserve to be special!" Sasha continued.

"Excuse me," Gina interrupted her. "I have to take this call. It's Zac's doctor."

She turned her back on Sasha as she answered the phone. "Doctor Carrini?"

"We tested Zac's blood for common household and environmental poisons that can make a person sick," Dr. Carrini said without preamble. "Nothing turned up. All his symptoms point to poison, but we're getting nowhere."

"And his condition has worsened," he continued. "Whatever this poison or toxin is, it's progressing quickly. It's affecting his kidneys."

Gina turned to look at Sasha, who still stood in a defensive pose. "What can you do?"

"The only option I have is to put him on dialysis," he said.

"Dialysis?" Gina said.

"It will flush his bloodstream and hopefully the toxin, too," the doctor said. "But it takes 48 hours for the body to be ready, and I'm concerned about possible kidney damage."

There was a long pause while Gina struggled to form a response. "Kidney damage?"

Sasha's face went white.

"That's assuming we can flush the toxin out," he said. "If we can't, well… his other organs will shut down too."

Gina nearly dropped the phone. "Are you saying he could die?" Across from her, Sasha made a strangled sound and clapped her hand over her mouth as if she were going to be ill.

"It's a remote possibility," he said. "Hold on a moment." There were muffled sounds of conversation on the doctor's end of the line. "I've got to go. We're going to prep Zac for dialysis right now."

"I'll get back there as soon as I can."

"Sounds good." He broke the connection.

Gina stood stock still for a long moment, trying to take in this new information. Then slowly she turned to Sasha.

Sasha's eyes were wide. "What is dialysis?" Her voice rose in pitch. "What are they doing to him?"

"They're trying to save his life," Gina said.

Sasha sat down hard on the bed as if she'd been slapped. "But that can't be!" she cried.

"I've got to get back to the hospital." Gina turned toward the door.

"I love him," Sasha wailed.

Without conscious awareness, Gina closed the space between herself and the younger woman. "Sasha, if you truly do love Zac then I need to know what happened the evening you spent in his room." She wanted to ask about cookies and mushrooms, but she didn't dare push that far.

She watched as Sasha's face went from tearful to a slightly blank look that actors used all the time. Gina knew it well, but it still made her stomach clench every time she saw it. *Because it was usually followed by a lie…*

"We had sex, that's what happened," Sasha spat. "I thought he loved me and wanted to get back together. But he said it was a mistake, that we couldn't be together. That he had outgrown me.

27

That he didn't want me anymore. And you know what? I don't want him, either."

Gina didn't know what to say. She straightened and looked at Dale. He just shrugged. The silence stretched out.

"So there's nothing else you want to tell me?" Gina finally said. *Like why you have information about poisonous mushrooms in your possession?*

"I want nothing to do with Zac Davies," Sasha sniffed, then stood. "And I want you out of my room!"

Gina continued to stare at the younger woman, but Sasha said nothing more, so Gina turned to go. She had her phone at her ear before the door closed behind her. In her haste she nearly bumped into Candy.

"I was right, wasn't I?" Candy said.

"You've got internet on your phone?"

"Yes."

Gina shoved the papers at her. "You're riding with me," she said. "Find out as much as you can about this mushroom while I drive...Hello? Gina Devereaux for Doctor Carrini, please. It's urgent. Yes, I know he's with a patient, it's that patient I need to talk to him about. Tell him I have information about the poison."

chapter 5

Doctor Carrini was waiting for Gina outside Zac's room. "You have a sample?"

Gina took the plastic bag from her purse. She held it gingerly, as if it were a living thing. A woman came around the corner. "That's it?" she said.

"Gina, this is Martha Jones," Doctor Carrini said. "She's a lab technician and she specializes in toxins."

Gina nodded to the technician. "Take what you need for testing. I want to keep the rest for the police."

Doctor Carrini looked at Gina. "Based on what you and your colleague told me about this substance, I'm afraid I have no choice but to place a catheter in Zac's jugular vein to administer immediate dialysis."

Gina barely suppressed a shudder, thankful that she'd insisted Candy wait in the lounge.

"It's a common procedure but not the best long-term solution for a young man like Zac," he said. "And it *will* be a long-term situation for him. He may need dialysis his entire life depending on how this goes."

Gina swallowed.

"I'll also be placing a graft in his left forearm," Doctor Carrini continued. "It creates what we call 'blood access' and is where the dialysis will take place in the future. Normally it takes the body a minimum of 48 hours to heal enough to conduct dialysis. At that point we can remove the jugular catheter."

"Is he unconscious for this?" Gina said.

"I'm hesitant to put him completely under," he said. "We'll use a combination of local anesthetics and sedatives."

A nurse balancing a tray of medical instruments brushed past them on her way into Zac's room. Despite never being the queasy type around blood, Gina's stomach clenched.

"If you want to ask him anything, you'd better do it now," Doctor Carrini said. "He may not be responsive by the time the police are ready to question him."

Gina looked back at him. "I'll need you present for that conversation, Doc."

Doctor Carrini nodded and held the door for her. She took a deep breath. She'd spent the better part of the drive trying to get her brain around what had happened. But she wasn't at all sure how much to tell Zac in the state he was in.

And when she saw him there, she nearly took a step back. He was so pale he looked gray, with a sheen of perspiration coating his face. Monitors were connected to his bare chest, the wires running up and over his shoulder. His left arm stuck straight out, strapped to a board, while his right lay limp at his side, an IV line embedded in it.

*   *   *   *   *   *   *   *   *   *   *   *   *

Zac heard his name as if from a long way off.

He turned his head toward the voice very slowly so as to minimize the dizziness. He cracked his eyes open. "Gina."

"Hey," she said. "I need to ask you some questions."

Was it his imagination, or did she look scared? Well, hell, he probably looked like a freak right now... "Sure."

"Sasha was in your room on Monday night, is that right?"

Monday night? Was that the day? "Yes."

"She brought you some cookies."

Where was she going with this? "How do you know...about the cookies?"

"Zac," she said. "I need to know how many cookies you ate that night and each day after that."

He closed his eyes as another wave of nausea washed over him. His fuzzy mind struggled to connect the questions. Was she implying...? "The cookies are making me sick?"

"It looks that way," she said.

Confusion swirled in his mind. "But... what? How...?"

"We don't know that yet," she said. "But it's really important we find out how many cookies you ingested since you got them."

"Jesus," he breathed.

He felt a hand slip into his. "Take your time," she said. "Concentrate."

Right.

"I had two that night," he said. "That's usually all I'll have... since I'm watching my weight."

"What about the next morning?"

He shook his head. Big mistake. Darkness pushed against the edges of his vision. He wasn't going to be able to do this...

"Okay," she said. "How about lunch or dinner that day?"

"Snack," he said. "Before sleep."

"How many?" she said.

"Two."

"Okay, that brings us to yesterday. Wednesday."

Something had happened on Wednesday…what was it?

"I missed breakfast," he muttered. "So I ate those. Two. And then, last night…" he trailed off. He was so tired; it would be so much easier to just let go…

"We had a tough shoot." Gina prompted him. "I asked you about doing drugs."

The crappy shoot…the conversation with Gina…feeling sick to his stomach…the headache…

Missing dinner…*Shit.*

"That was dinner," he said. "Don't know how many…the rest… almost gone…" The darkness was pressing on all sides now.

"How many is that?" Zac heard the doctor but couldn't answer him. He was falling, falling, falling into darkness…

And Gina's voice: "Too many."

*   *   *   *   *   *   *   *   *   *   *   *   *

As soon as the others had left, Gina slipped into Zac's room. The lights had been turned down and the dialysis machine's computer screen gave the room an eerie quality. Gauze covered Zac's neck and right shoulder area. Tubes tinted blood-red ran from the dialysis machine and disappeared under the gauze.

The thin hospital sheets bunched up around his waist, and his left arm was bandaged from elbow to wrist. "Oh Zac…" she breathed.

The low whir and beep of the machine and the steady rise of Zac's chest calmed her. But as she lowered herself toward him, she noticed a sheen of perspiration across his forehead. Without thinking, she reached out one hand and laid it against his forehead.

"Miss Devereaux." The voice behind her was quiet but it still caused her heart to lurch into her chest.

"Doc," Gina said without looking up. "He's running a fever."

"Yes," he said. "One hundred one point nine at the moment."

Gina looked at him then.

"Fever is the body's way of fighting off illness," he said. "It's a good sign. We're keeping close tabs on it and will bring it down if it gets too high."

They both fell silent.

Finally she spoke. "I should have brought him in earlier, when he first passed out."

"I'm not sure it would have changed anything that happened," he said. "It seemed the toxin took a while to really affect him, but when it did, it was very fast. I'm frankly amazed at your super-sleuth act."

"It didn't keep him off dialysis," she said.

"I don't think anything would have." He moved to stand across from her.

"Is having the cookies any help?"

"Most of the damage had been done already," he said. "But knowing more about this substance will help him recover more quickly."

She bit her lip, afraid to ask about the ongoing nature of dialysis.

"Why don't you go and get some rest?" he said.

Doctor Carrini was right. There was nothing she could do here. She stood.

At that moment Zac moaned.

Gina's breathing stopped. "Zac?"

"Mom... Dad...." Zac's adams apple bobbed as if he were having trouble swallowing. He moaned again. And then... silence.

Gina glanced at Doctor Carrini. He was staring intently at the digital readouts above the bed. A light came on above her, causing her to blink in the brightness, and a nurse appeared beside the doctor.

The silence was broken by Zac's ragged voice. "Mom! Dad! Oh no! Oh God!"

His hand moved, as if to grasp at something. "Please no... *don't!*"

Gina dropped back into the chair and grabbed his hand in hers. He pulled on it with surprising strength. "You don't know..." Now he tried to move his legs. "You don't know what they're going to do to you!"

"No!" He cried out, as if frustrated with his inability to move. "Mom! Dad!"

His hand dropped, all strength gone from it. "No..."

His voice faded to a mournful cry that put Gina's teeth on edge. "Noooo..."

Gina looked up at Doctor Carrini. "I think it's time to bring the temp down."

The doctor nodded. He turned to speak to the nurse, but Gina wasn't listening. She was staring at Zac's face.

He was crying.

chapter 6

Zac opened his eyes to find himself staring at a bland ceiling. *Shouldn't I be in my hotel room?*

He started to turn his head but something was pricking him in the right side of his neck. He raised his right arm, intending to touch his neck, but pain shot through his neck and shoulder and he dropped his hand quickly. He noticed there was an IV in his wrist. *What the—?*

He lifted his left arm, only to discover it was wrapped in a bandage from elbow to wrist. His pulse quickened, accompanied by a dull pain in both his neck and his arm. He was so weak; it felt as though all the blood had rushed from his body…

Dread settled in the pit of his stomach.

All the blood had *left his body…*

Carefully he brought his hand to his neck. It too had a bandage on it, but it was loose and he easily worked his fingers underneath it. Felt the smooth surface of a tube…or maybe two. Gingerly he followed the tubing until…it disappeared into his skin.

He yanked his hand away as if he'd touched fire. These tubes were…inside him??

Oh my God, it had really happened. Passing out…being sick in Gina's car…tubes down his throat… the terrible pain as his neck was *cut...it was all **real**.*

His throat closed in on itself, and he screwed his eyes shut against a sudden onslaught of nausea. He fought to bring his breathing under control. Tried to remember...

Cookies. Gina asked about cookies...and Sasha.

He needed to talk to Gina. He opened his eyes, intending to find the call button. Instead his eyes met those of a man who'd just entered the room. He wore a white coat.

"Hello Zac," the man said. "I'm Doctor Carrini. I treated you when you arrived yesterday."

"I remember you." Zac's voice was so scratchy it was almost a whisper. "What's in my neck? And why is it there?"

"It's a catheter," Doctor Carrini said. "It gives us direct access to your vein. It was placed there as an emergency measure to allow us to clean your blood. It's called dialysis."

Zac could only stare at him.

"You ingested a poisonous substance that has affected your liver function," the doctor said. "We need to talk about what this means."

*   *   *   *   *   *   *   *   *   *   *   *   *

It had been a restless night and Gina arrived at the hospital early. She was looking for Doctor Carrini; instead she found Sylvester and Gerri standing just outside the nurse's station. "Gina," Sylvester said. "I'm glad you're here. Please join us in the visitor room for a meeting."

Gina dutifully followed Gerri while Sylvester ordered one of the nurses to find Doctor Carrini. Zac's agent was already seated at the table, as was Sylvester's public relations guy, Kurt. *Of course.* She sighed with resignation; she was going to be stuck in this meeting when all she really wanted to do was see Zac.

"Coffee?" Gerri asked.

Gina shook her head.

"Have we reached Zac's guardians yet?" Sylvester said as he entered the room.

"Not yet," Gerri said.

"Guardians?" Gina asked.

"His aunt and uncle," the agent said. "Zac's parents died fourteen years ago."

Gina's spine went rigid.

"Zac was fifteen and an only child," the agent said. "He was sent to live with an aunt and uncle in Florida, but by all accounts he was just marking time until he could leave for college."

"His parents," Gina said. "How did they die?"

Gerri looked down at a manila folder in front of her. "Violently."

Gina felt sick to her stomach. Before she could respond, Doctor Carrini entered. He looked as if he'd slept in his clothes. His hair was a bit wild and there were deep lines around his eyes. His eyes met hers briefly and he nodded. Gerri offered him coffee, which he accepted.

"Doctor," Sylvester said. "Please give us an update on Mister Davies' condition."

"Zac is awake," Doctor Carrini said. "But he's woozy and disoriented, which is to be expected. The police are questioning him now. The main concern at the moment is dizziness and nausea, which seem to come and go. And, of course, the damage to his liver."

"What is the prognosis?" Sylvester sounded sanguine, but Gina could pick up his agitated vibe from across the table.

"The poison did some damage to his kidneys; he's probably going to need dialysis three times a week in the short term. He may need it once or twice a week for the foreseeable future. He'll likely be prone to sudden dizzy spells for awhile. He cannot be left alone for a couple weeks."

Discussing Zac without him there seemed an invasion of privacy to Gina, especially without a family member present. "Does Zac know this yet?"

Doctor Carrini nodded at Gina. "He does."

Before Gina could follow up on that thought, Sylvester broke in. "When can he return to work?"

The doctor turned to Sylvester. "By work, I assume you mean acting in your film?"

Sylvester looked irritated. "Yes, Doctor."

"That depends on what he is physically required to do," Doctor Carrini said. "There may be some limitations. But given he's young and healthy—and *if* he can give himself a true recovery period—he might be able to ease into things in two to three weeks, as long as the work schedule accommodates dialysis sessions." He looked pointedly at Sylvester.

"What do you mean by a 'true' recovery period?" Gina asked.

The doctor turned to her again. "He needs to be in a safe, quiet place," he said. "Initially, he'll need someone with him at all times. Imagine if he had a dizzy spell and fell. No stressors. No responsibilities. No physical activity beyond a short walk. And no driving for at least two weeks."

"Given that we've yet to hear from his closest relatives, I would guess they may not be able to provide that," Gerri said.

"You might consider hospice care," Doctor Carrini said. "Or our Extended Care Residency service."

"Thank you, doctor." Sylvester said in a tone that indicated he was excused.

To his credit, Doctor Carrini continued. "A young man like Mister Davies is used to being self-sufficient. He may not like the idea of others taking care of him. He may resist, or even insist he doesn't need it." The doctor's eyes flickered to Gina's. "Unless it's presented in the proper way."

The proper way…what would that be?

Apparently Sylvester thought he knew. "Zac will understand it's a direct order, Doctor."

Doctor Carrini stood. "I'll discuss it with my patient."

As soon as he was gone, Sylvester said, "We need to decide what we're going to tell the public—not to mention the crew. We can't give them the impression any of our cast has been taking drugs. Kurt?"

Of course, Gina thought. *The OD.*

A famous actor had overdosed and died on the set of Sylvester's last production. The resulting accusations and media frenzy had cost Sylvester dearly…

"What about a replacement?" the PR guy said.

Gina caught Sylvester's gaze and held it.

"Zac stays," Sylvester said.

Kurt sighed. "The media is going to find out Zac is in the hospital—if they haven't already. I think we should stick to the food poisoning story. It will just have to be handled carefully. If we craft the message right, we can even use it to our advantage—turn it into more PR for the film. What we don't want is Zac's story to overshadow the film's PR."

Gina was getting uneasy with the conversation.

"And Zac?" the agent said.

"I understand he was in possession of Vicodin?" Kurt said.

"That was doctor-prescribed," Gina said. "For a previous injury."

"But he was using it for a different purpose than originally intended," Kurt said.

Gina didn't have a response for that.

"To be sure the story is consistent, I think it's best if we keep Mister Davies out of reach of the public," Kurt said. "We need to control access to him. If we let him go home, we can't do that. He might say something we don't want him to say, even if inadvertently."

"So hospice care is out," Sylvester said. "If the guardians step up, they'll have to take him elsewhere."

Gina couldn't believe what she was hearing. "He can't go to his own *home*?"

Kurt turned to her. "If the reporters get wind of this story, he'll have no peace at home, which would undermine his recovery."

"Assuming his guardians don't step up, that leaves Extended Care," Gerri said.

"It may cost you," Kurt addressed Sylvester, "but it's the best way to control the message."

The best way to control the "message" … or to control Zac?

"Excuse me," Gina said, "but has anyone asked *Zac* what he'd like to do?"

Sylvester gave her one of his cold stares. "If Zac wants to keep his job, he'll do as we say. Now let's talk about what this means to the production schedule…"

*   *   *   *   *   *   *   *   *   *   *   *   *

Gina was further detained by the police, who wanted to get her side of the story. At least now she knew that Sasha was in police custody and her room being thoroughly searched. But it took Gina several minutes of concerted effort to calm herself after that. She looked for Doctor Carrini, but when she didn't find him, she decided she wasn't waiting any longer. She knocked on the door to Zac's room, and when there was no answer she let herself in.

Zac looked considerably better than he had yesterday. But then, that wasn't saying much. A hospital gown now covered his shoulders and chest. The tubes were gone, though the gauze on his neck remained, hiding the catheter.

Gina stepped to the window and stood looking out, trying to imagine what it must have been like for Zac, to lose his parents like that. He'd been the same age Christine was now... why hadn't she known?

Then again, why would she? It wasn't exactly a topic that came up during an audition. And she guessed it wasn't a subject Zac brought up much at all. They were co-workers, nothing more. Temporary ones, at that. It was the nature of the business; paths crossed for a short time, then continued on their own ways.

Gina's mind drifted to Zac's third audition.

She'd asked him what interested him most about the wounded veteran character he was auditioning for. Instead of the usual answer about the challenge or the opportunity to stretch himself, he'd mentioned a friend, a real-life soldier who had just returned from Iraq. And unless her bullshit radar had been off that day, his answer was heartfelt.

She remembered thinking: *he just might have that inner something to really make this part soar.*

Then she'd asked him why he chose to be an actor.

His response had been immediate, like it had slipped out before he'd thought about it fully. "When I'm acting, I'm living someone else's life."

"Is there something wrong with yours?" she'd asked.

Zac hesitated. "I think everyone has had times in their life when they wish they were someone else. Haven't you?"

She sensed that familiar *hunger* that so many actors had. Heck, she *wanted* her actors to be hungry. But had she misinterpreted Zac's? Was it possible that his hunger was, in fact... a deep pain?

"Gina?"

She startled at the sound of his voice. "Hey." She turned and lowered herself into a chair that had been left by his bed. "How are you feeling?"

"I'm…" His blue-green eyes seemed to dim and lose focus. He winced as he ran a hand through his hair. "I feel like I've been run over by a truck."

She sensed he had more to say, so she waited.

"The police were here," he said. "They asked a million questions about Sasha. About our relationship… I just can't…" his voice trailed off.

"Can't get your head around it?" She was feeling that way too, but she didn't say it aloud.

"I mean, why would she…" He shuddered, then pressed a hand to his head. "Maybe it wasn't her…you know?"

"Well, she hasn't confessed," Gina said.

"But you found the cookies." He looked at her for the first time.

"That's true," she said. "But I had to go through your stuff. Sorry about that."

He stared at her. "She was upset…"

"That much seems obvious," Gina said.

"Not that night," he said. "The week before, when we…after we…"

"When you what?" she said. "Spit it out, Zac."

"Ah, hell," he sighed. "We ran into each other out on the town. I was drinking…she came onto me, said just once for old times sake and…we did. I realized it was a mistake. I talked to her about it. She seemed okay."

"Zac," Gina said. "Most women are not okay with a one-night-stand and a blow-off from the man they're in love with."

"In—what?"

Gina stood. "In love, Zac. She was in love with you."

"What we had was not *love*."

"Maybe to her it was," Gina said. "Wait. Did you say this was the week before?"

"That's right," he said.

"You didn't have sex Monday night?"

Zac looked at her quizzically. "No. Why?"

"She made it sound like you slept together the same night she gave you the cookies," Gina said.

"No," he said firmly. "I wasn't about to make that mistake again."

"But what if she really believes you did that night?"

Zac opened his mouth to say something, but before he could the phone on his bedside stand rang.

chapter 7

"Zac, is that you?"

He recognized the voice at once. *Of course they would have been called.* "Yes, Aunt Trudy, it's me."

"Thank goodness!" she said. "Those hospital people got me all turned around trying to find you. What is going on? The messages said something about you being poisoned."

"It's… it's just bad food, Aunt Trudy." Zac caught a glimpse of Gina's raised brow.

"Bad food?" she said. "Aren't you on that photo shoot? What kind of production feeds you bad food? They made it sound like more than that. Goodness, the messages I got made it sound like you were on your deathbed!"

He suddenly felt woozy and sick to his stomach. "I was pretty sick," he said, "but I'm on the mend now."

"Maybe I should come…"

"No!" Zac said quickly, trying to tamp down the dizziness and nausea. "It's not necessary. Really." The crisis was over, after all, and he could tell from the hesitation in her voice that she didn't really want to leave Florida. He called on his acting ability. "I'll be fine."

"Well, you're a grown man and I suppose you can take care

of yourself," she said. "You would tell me if you needed me, wouldn't you?"

"Yes, Aunt Trudy."

They chatted a few more minutes and he excused himself.

When he hung up, he found Gina looking at him with open curiosity. "You don't want her to know?"

He shrugged.

"Why?" she said.

"She's ten years older than my mom, and they never got along," Zac said. "She and my uncle never wanted kids, didn't really know what to do with one, and then suddenly they were stuck with a moody teenager they'd never really known. They've done enough."

Gina's gaze didn't waver. "Surely they didn't blame you for being 'moody' considering you'd just lost your parents."

He looked at her sharply.

"Yeah, we all know," she said. "No privacy in a hospital."

"Terrific," he muttered. "What did Sylvester say?"

"He's busy figuring out how to put a good PR spin on the whole thing, of course."

"He's not planning on telling the whole world about my parents, is he?"

"On the contrary," she said. "He wants to keep everything that happened here mum."

"Well," he said. "We actually agree on something. At least he's not talking about firing me."

"He won't fire you," she said. "You're doing a fine job. I'm sorry about your mom and dad."

"It was a long time ago."

*   *   *   *   *   *   *   *   *   *   *   *   *

Zac stared at a piece of lint on the blanket, and Gina couldn't help but re-live the night before when he'd cried out to his dead parents. Did he dream of them often?

"Zac?" she said. "Has Doctor Carrini talked to you about what happens next?"

He sucked in a breath. "Dialysis three times a week. Dizzy spells, nausea. He said I can't be alone for the next week. I can't even *drive* for two weeks."

"Has he said anything about *where* you're going to recover?"

"Home, I assume," he said.

"I'm afraid Sylvester is going to veto that," she said. "You remember a couple years ago, that actor who overdosed on his set?"

"I remember," he said. "But what's that got to do with me?"

"Well, the PR guru is concerned about the fact that Vicodin was in your possession."

"But that's not like that cokehead that died," he said. "That was just leftover medication, prescribed by a doctor."

"Doesn't matter," she said. "If the paparazzi find out about it, they'll make it sound like something—shall we say less *legal*—was in your bag."

She watched as comprehension spread across his features. "Shit! I can't go home, can I?"

"I suspect Sylvester is going to insist you stay in Extended Care."

"In solitary confinement," he said.

"It's not like that."

He looked at her, and she sighed. "Okay. It is like that."

They fell silent.

"You know, you do have a choice," she said. "Sylvester doesn't own you."

"But he does." The bitterness in Zac's voice surprised her. "At least for now. He'll make sure I know it if he wants me to do something."

Gina wanted to say something about how Sylvester wasn't that bad once you knew him…but she didn't. She couldn't. Not after his reaction to the past day's events…

"You could stay at my place." The words out of her own mouth startled her.

His eyebrows shot up.

"I've got a little piece of land outside L.A.," she said. "We call it the ranchette. Nothing fancy, but it does have a guest room."

Zac was staring at her.

"The nanny stays there when I'm on location, and takes care of my girls," she continued. "I'm pretty sure we can convince Sylvester it's far enough and remote enough."

Zac continued to stare.

"Of course, the offer also includes two rather boisterous teenage girls."

Why am I rambling?

Finally he spoke. "Are you sure, Gina? After all, you hardly know me."

That was true. *But didn't she?*

Before she could formulate a response, there was another tap on his door. Zac's agent poked his head in.

"Howard," Zac said.

Gina backed up, suddenly feeling the need to flee. "I'll leave you two to talk. I'll check in with you later…"

* * * * * * * * * * * * *

Howard's news confirmed Gina's; Zac still had the part, thank God.

For now.

But only if he refused to talk to the media...and spent his recovery time in seclusion.

Zac didn't know what he'd do if he didn't act. It was what he'd been doing the night his parents died...

Zac tried to sleep, but his arm and neck and shoulder were throbbing, a side effect Doctor Carrini had failed to mention. Every time he'd doze off, he would dream... bizarre, nonsensical dreams that he couldn't quite recall upon waking. He had a vague sense of his parents coming to him, as if trying to deliver a message. The dreams were disconcerting, since he made a conscious effort not to dwell on his parents.

He turned his thoughts to Gina. Under other circumstances, he probably would have labeled her nosy for even mentioning his parents. But for some reason he felt her interest was genuine, rather than the morbid fascination people usually reacted with. At least, the few people he'd told. As a general rule, that was privileged information.

What to make of her offer? Was she making it because she felt responsible for what had happened to him? He had to admit it was appealing. He could spend his time confined to a sick bed and cut off from everyone, or he could be free to move about in the...countryside?...and *still* be cut off from everyone.

Except...

The thought of being around Gina and her girls felt oddly comforting. Less lonely? He pondered that; it was an unaccustomed feeling. As he finally dropped into sleep he made his decision: if the offer still stood when he saw Gina again, he would take it.

chapter 8

Gina stepped off the elevator and checked her watch. Zac was probably chomping at the bit by now.

The door to Zac's room was open. Just before she reached it she heard Doctor's Carrini's voice. "When I say the word, Zac, I want you to take a deep breath, then hold it."

Her hand froze on the door frame. Hesitantly she peeked around it. The doctor and a nurse had their backs to her as they leaned over Zac. The bed had been raised and a bright light focused on the area of his neck. All she could see of Zac was his legs, one knee bent almost casually.

"And…now," Doctor Carrini said. "And…hold."

Zac's leg twitched.

"It's coming out…" Gina couldn't see "it" but she knew it was the catheter.

Zac's breath came out on a barely contained moan. "Sonofabitch, that burns!" he gasped.

Instinctively Gina took a step toward him. Then she caught herself.

He might not want me to see this.

And yet she couldn't look away.

"It's out." Doctor Carrini handed something to the nurse, but Gina's attention was drawn to Zac's lower body. His legs moved against the bed in a motion Gina recognized from her days of coaching soccer…a coping mechanism for pain.

"I have to tell you, Doc, that numbing stuff doesn't do shit." Zac's voice was terse.

"It will help with the stitches," the doctor said.

"Stitches?"

"Just a half-dozen or so," Doctor Carrini said.

"Great," Zac muttered. "Is that going to leave a scar?"

"Not if I do it right."

Zac turned his head to look at the doctor, and Gina got the slightest glimpse of his face when he flinched from the movement. Hastily she stepped away from the door.

"Relax, Zac," Doctor Carrini said. "I've done about a million stitches in my career. You've got nothing to worry about."

Gina glanced up and down the hallway to see if anyone had noticed her. Thankfully it was deserted and the nurses were all away from the central station. She heard Doctor Carrini's voice as she backed away from the door. "Nancy will dress this for you," he was saying. "And I'll go sign off on your chart so you can leave as soon as your ride is here."

Gina was standing by the elevator when Doctor Carrini came out of Zac's room. "Miss Devereaux," he said. "I was hoping to have a chance to talk to you…alone."

"Certainly."

He waved at the small room that served as a family area; then followed her into the room.

"How has he been?" Gina had gotten a couple updates from Gerri but they'd been short on detail.

"I'd say he's done better than expected," Doctor Carrini said.

"But there are some things I need you to be aware of."

He rested one hip on the edge of the couch. "What Zac's mostly been experiencing this week is headaches—some severe—as well as dizziness and the nausea that goes along with that. Those things are likely part of the poison moving within his system, but they've been exacerbated by the fact that we've had a difficult time keeping his blood pressure steady. He has medication for his blood pressure; if you can, please encourage him to take it."

"He also has Vicodin for pain management," he continued. "Though I doubt he'll use it."

"Why do you say that?" Had he forgotten Zac had taken Vicodin before becoming so sick?

"After so many years of being a doctor, I can usually tell those patients that have an aversion to drugging themselves—it goes hand-in-hand with an aversion to doctors in general." He chuckled. "And as I mentioned before, Zac is a young and otherwise healthy man, and he isn't going to like the fact that he needs to rely on someone else's help for a while."

"I'm a little concerned about that myself," Gina said.

"You strike me as someone with just the right gentle-yet-firm personality he needs right now," he said. "And you've offered a place that's free of pressure in which to recuperate, which is key. If you can just keep him quiet for a week I think we'll find he's made a vast improvement."

Gina felt her face grow warm. "Is there anything I need to know about the dialysis?"

"I think that's all arranged," he said. "The lab in Silver Springs is going to keep me updated, and I'll see him in two weeks when you're back."

"Will he be strong enough?" she said. "To work? His job isn't easy, no matter what it looks like. I wouldn't want him to have any setbacks."

"I hope so," he said. "Because your boss doesn't sound like he's going to wait longer than that." He stood. "But he'll have to provide time for Zac to get to dialysis, because if he misses that he will get very sick. Life-and-death sick."

chapter 9

Darkness was falling when Gina entered Zac's room. He was propped up in bed wearing gym pants and a white T-shirt, watching the nurse wrap his arm.

"Thank God!" He said. "You're late."

"Blame it on Doctor Carrini." Her eyes were drawn to the gauze bandage on his neck.

As if in response, his hand went to his neck. But before he could say anything the nurse spoke. "I'm going to get you a supply of these bandages to take with you."

Zac waited for her to leave the room. "Get me out of here," he said.

He looked as if he hadn't slept much. His hair was tousled and he sported several days' worth of beard stubble. But it was his eyes that told her how truly miserable he'd been; normally vibrant and startling, they were flat and... *exhausted* was the only word that came to mind.

"Are you packed?" she said.

He nodded toward a gym bag. "Mack brought me a few things from home."

"Mack?"

"He's the friend I told you about," he said. "The one who

recently came back from Iraq. He also hooked me up with a lawyer."

"Hmm," she said. He had said that so casually; did she dare ask how he felt about Sasha being released from custody?

"The computer is the only thing I really care about," he continued. "And I've already had my exit interview."

Gina smiled at his choice of words. She picked up his computer and tucked it into the bag as the nurse sat down to finish bandaging Zac's arm.

"So you have all the paperwork done and things lined up in Silver Springs?" Gina said.

He nodded. "Gerri did a lot of it. Seems Sylvester's name carries weight even out there."

"More like his pocketbook," she muttered.

"Here you go." The nurse handed Zac a faded blue long-sleeve button-up shirt. "I put all your meds in your bag. All you need to do is sign some discharge papers."

"Thanks." Zac slipped his left arm into the sleeve gingerly. Gina stepped to the bed and held the other sleeve for him. He winced when he had to move his arm backward. He didn't bother with the buttons.

The nurse parked a wheelchair next to his bed and he slipped into it without comment.

"Why don't I bring the car around?" Gina said.

"We'll meet you at the entrance," the nurse said.

*   *   *   *   *   *   *   *   *   *   *   *   *

Zac carefully maneuvered his body into the passenger seat, then turned to look at the suitcase in the back seat. "Is that all my stuff from the hotel?"

"I hope so," Gina said. "Dale packed, so I have no idea if

everything is there."

"Hmm." He faced forward and reached for the seatbelt as the car began to move.

"In a day or two when you're more rested, we can go into town and get you some extra shirts or whatever you might need," she said.

Go into town. It almost made him smile.

He sighed deeply, sinking into the seat. "If I haven't said it…" He rubbed his arms, suddenly chilled. "I really appreciate you opening up your home to me."

She turned her head to look at him intently. Her eyes were a dark chocolate brown, same as her hair. Why had he never noticed before? "I hope you'll be comfortable there. Would you like a blanket? There should be one of Allie's in the back seat."

"Oh I—"

How did she know?

Well, he wasn't going to turn it down. He twisted in his seat to retrieve the blanket. As soon as he'd draped it over himself, drowsiness set in. His eyelids drooped. "The hospital is *not* a restful place," he muttered.

"Why don't you close your eyes and get some of the rest you've missed out on?" she said. "I won't be offended."

"Hmm," he said. "I might just do that…"

He woke as they pulled up to a gas pump. "Where are we?"

"Only about twenty minutes from home," Gina said. "We need gas. You want anything? Water or bathroom break?"

"I'm fine, thanks."

It felt odd to sit while she pumped the gas, but he felt weak and stiff, and his arm and neck were throbbing.

He watched as she crossed the tarmac to the convenience store. He dug a water bottle and Tylenol out of his gym bag and washed a couple pills down. His body craved a quiet place with a real bed…and some time alone to process everything that had happened in the last week.

When they were on the road again, he said, "So you have two daughters."

"Two teenagers, so prepare yourself now." She smiled. "Christine just turned fifteen, and Allie is thirteen."

"What are they like?"

"Christine is the studious type," Gina said. "She's shy and she likes things in their place. She's logical and a bit of a perfectionist. Allie, on the other hand, is the family dramatist. Everything is a big emotional thing to her. She's also a great singer and artist."

"An actor in the making?" he said.

She glanced at him. "If that's what she wants to do, I'll support her. But I hope she doesn't."

"Why?"

She shrugged. "It's a difficult career, especially for women. So what do you do for relaxation?"

Although Zac was curious about her aversion to his profession, he was too tired to pursue it. "I like to surf."

He caught a glimpse of a smile in the darkened car. "A true California boy, are you?"

"L.A. born and bred," he said. "Mack and I spent all our time on the beach. We've tried every beach along the California coast, and some in Oregon too."

"You've been friends a long time then?"

"Since third grade," he said. "God, the things we got into…my parents used to call us the *Mack and Zac Attack*."

"Do you still surf?"

"Not so much," he said. "Mack was in the service. Spent a couple years in Iraq. He only recently got out. And I've been either working or going to auditions. So how about you? When you're not directing or parenting, what do you like to do?"

"I ride my Harley."

"Really?" He couldn't hide the surprise in his voice. "You're a biker chick?"

She laughed, and he liked the sound of it. "Yep."

"So let me ask you something I've always been curious about," he said. "What is it about riding a motorcycle that is so appealing?"

"You obviously haven't ridden one."

"Mack's got a scooter," he said. "But that's about the extent of my exposure to motorcycles."

"That's not a motorcycle," she teased.

He shrugged.

"Let me put it this way," she said. "What is it about surfing that you like?"

"Well," he said. "It's the salt against your skin…the wind in your hair…the way your stomach lifts with the wave. It's hard to explain; you have to experience it for yourself. There's a certain… freedom in it."

"A-ha!" She pointed at him. "You understand more than you think."

"That's not the same as experiencing it for yourself," he said.

"True," she said. "But now I *know* you'd like the motorcycle."

He couldn't help it; he yawned. "Wow," he mumbled. "A Harley-riding girl director… who'd have thought?"

He must have dozed off again, because the next thing he knew, they were pulling into the driveway of a long ranch-style home. The outside lights were on.

"Home sweet home." Gina cut the motor.

Zac willed himself to open the door. He stood, feeling unsteady on his feet. Moving carefully, he closed the front door and opened the back door as Gina came around the rear of the car. He bent over to retrieve his suitcase, and a wave of dizziness washed over him, so strong it threatened to topple him. He gripped the edge of the car as his vision tunneled.

This is not good.

"Zac?" Gina's hand came to rest in the small of his back.

His body trembled with the effort of keeping a grip on consciousness. Of not allowing his legs to buckle beneath him.

She felt it.

Her other hand came up and she wrapped both hands around his sides, bringing her body closer to his. "Easy, Zac."

He fought for control, his breath coming in shaky gulps. His fingers gripped the edge of the car frame and his head rested against the hood.

"Arrrrgh!" He slapped his hand against the hood of the car in frustration.

"Zachariah." Her voice was soft, but he was still startled by the use of his full name. "You just got out of the hospital. Your body has been through a lot. Give it time; you'll be okay."

Nothing about this is okay, he wanted to shout. *I have tubes in my arm. They freakin' pulled all my blood out and put it back again. I have kidney damage, and I may have to do this dialysis thing the rest of my life...*

But he couldn't say any of it.

"I know you're used to doing everything for yourself," she continued. "But please let me help with the bags."

She was right, of course. He drew in a careful breath; at least he hadn't fainted.

"You can make it up to me later by fixing my faucet or painting the chicken coop," she said.

"You have a *chicken coop*?" He would have laughed if he'd felt better.

"It's a 4H project gone awry." She chuckled. "Though they are hilarious little creatures. Excellent eggs, too."

She let the silence fall, and all Zac could think about was how through-and-through exhausted he was. So tired, in fact, that he wondered if he could stand without Gina's presence against his back. "Go ahead with the bags," he finally said. "I'll wait here."

He felt her presence shift and lifted his head to meet her eyes.

Apparently she was satisfied with what she saw there. "All right."

Zac breathed in cool, clean air. In front of him, a low mountain range lay in shadows, dark blue ridge upon ridge. It was stunning, even in the dark. Gingerly he tilted his head to look at the sky. A thousand stars winked down on him, each one like a miniature beacon. He couldn't recall ever seeing stars as big and bright as these…

He felt Gina's presence return to his side. "Beautiful, isn't it?"

"It is," he breathed.

"Shall we?" She offered him her arm.

He squared his shoulders, then linked his arm through hers. "We shall."

*　　*　　*　　*　　*　　*　　*　　*　　*　　*　　*　　*　　*

"Guest bedroom." Gina released Zac's arm as he entered the room. "Bathroom is right across the hall. Everything else can wait until you've gotten some sleep."

Zac had stumbled slightly on the front steps. Though she'd said nothing, Gina was alarmed at how weak he seemed after that dizzy spell—or whatever it was—in her driveway. Now he crossed the room and stood at the window.

"I've got to go out back and check on the chickens," she said.

He nodded. "Gina."

"Yes?"

"Thank you."

"You're welcome."

She heard him in the bathroom as she let herself out the back deck.

She wasn't out there more than ten minutes. She checked in on Christine and Allie; they were sleeping soundly. The house was silent, yet the guest bedroom door was slightly ajar and the small table lamp was still on.

What if Zac had fallen or fainted?

She peeked through the slot in the door. Zac lay sprawled on the bed, motionless. He still wore the T-shirt and gym pants, even his shoes. She pushed against the door. "Zac?" she said softly.

There was no response.

She crossed the room and knelt beside him. She was relieved to see his chest rise and fall steadily. She studied the shadows the lamp cast on his face. The man was just plain exhausted. Very gently she ran her fingers over the bandage on this left arm.

She moved to the foot of the bed and untied his shoelaces. Gingerly she slipped off first one shoe, then the other. He didn't move a muscle, so she did the same with his socks.

Then she was stuck. He'd flipped the covers back but much of his body weight held them in place. Nights got cold; she would have to risk waking him to get him covered.

She managed to work the sheet and blanket from under his legs without moving him. It got trickier as she moved up his body. Finally she decided she'd just have to pull them out from under him in one swift motion.

When she did, his bandaged arm jerked and his body tensed. He mumbled something that faded into kind of a whisper. "It's okay, Zac," she whispered as she pulled the covers over him. His body relaxed and he shifted position, but he didn't wake.

Gina tiptoed to the door. "Good night, Zac," she murmured.

chapter 10

Zac blinked, trying to chase the fog of sleep away. He was still wearing the T-shirt and pants from yesterday. Memory returned: Gina's house. He had managed to brush his teeth, use the toilet, and shuck off his long-sleeve shirt before falling onto the blessedly firm bed.

He ran his right hand down his left arm, feeling the bumps where the graft was embedded in his vein. *Guess that wasn't just a bad dream.*

He heard the clinking of dishes and low voices, and rolled over to check the clock on the bedside stand. 5:12. Surely that wasn't P.M. —was it?

The slant of the sun outside the shaded window told him it was. That would mean he'd slept for over 16 hours! Now his bladder was telling him it was true.

Gingerly he stood and crossed the hallway to use the bathroom. Then he followed the sounds to the kitchen area.

"Oh my gosh, you're here!" A girl jumped up from the table and threw her arms around him. "You're really here!"

He chuckled self-consciously. "I guess you don't mind having me. You must be…"

"I'm Allie," she said. "And that's my big sister Christine."

"We have visitors fairly often," Christine said. "Lots of overnights for mom's work. None as famous as you, though."

"Famous?" he said. "I think you've got me confused with someone else." He glanced at Gina. It was odd seeing her in a kitchen, making dinner. Like a normal parent…

"Now that introductions are done," Gina said, "Do you have an appetite at all? Tonight's fare is chicken cordon bleu."

To his surprise, he felt as though he could actually eat a little something. "I'd like that," he said. "Though I should probably shower…"

"Eat first," Gina said as she placed a hotplate on the table. "Or it may be gone when you get here."

His mouth watered and when Allie said, "Sit here, Zac!" he did.

"You do kind of smell like a hospital," Allie said.

"Allie!" Christine said.

"I sort of still feel like that, too," Zac said. "Sorry."

"It's okay," Allie said. "After what you've been through and all, we understand."

"Hmm." How much did these girls of Gina's know?

"We can show you all the bathroom stuff after dinner," Allie continued.

Gina sat in the seat across from him. "Grace," she said.

Zac was surprised when Allie grabbed his hand. Then he realized Christine was waiting for him to take hers as well. When he did, the girls bowed their heads. He followed their lead, sitting quietly as they said a prayer. Something about the prayer was familiar; a long-forgotten memory flittered just out of reach.

"Well, you might not be famous yet." Allie spooned green beans onto her plate. "But mom says we have to all agree on a story for why you're here."

"Um, Allie…" Gina said.

"So the story is, you're our second cousin's friend," Allie said. "You got robbed in Mexico, drank bad water, and needed a place to stay."

He raised his eyebrows. "Really? You got it all figured out, huh?"

He glanced at Gina, but she just shrugged and said, "I'm not sure about the robbed part."

"Well, how else do you explain that he has no money?" Allie said.

"You've got a point there," Gina said.

"Hmm," Zac said. "Maybe I was scuba diving in Mexico and lost my wallet?"

Allie appeared to consider that. "Not nearly as exciting."

Zac couldn't help chuckling; Gina had been right about Allie's imagination. "Okay," he said, "but I hope no one asks too many questions about Mexico, since I've never been there!"

*　*　*　*　*　*　*　*　*　*　*　*　*

Gina had just finished going through the mail when Zac re-entered the kitchen area. He looked like he'd showered more than just the hospital smell away. For the first time since Gina had known him, he looked … relaxed. Although she could see he'd knicked himself with the blade in at least one place, and she couldn't help wondering if dizziness had anything to do with it.

"So what is this I hear about a chicken coop?" he said.

"Oh, you have to see it!" Christine said.

Zac glanced at Gina; she just chuckled and waved her hand.

She watched as the girls led Zac across the yard. She hoped she wasn't setting a bad example by stretching the truth about Zac's presence in their home. She had promised Sylvester she wouldn't tell anyone who Zac really was. But from a personal standpoint, she didn't want any of her neighbors to think Zac was anything more than a temporary visitor. If it came to that, she'd be forced to let the cat out of the bag. She certainly didn't need any gossip about her love life again...

Three hours later Gina kissed her girls goodnight and walked back through the living area. Zac wasn't there, and her stomach tightened with worry.

How ridiculous. He's a grown man.

She doubled back to check the guest room. Empty.

What if he'd gone somewhere and had another dizzy spell like the one last night?

She went back through the living area into the kitchen. He wasn't there, either. With a growing sense of worry, she pushed through the back door to the deck.

Zac looked up from where he sat on one of the deck chairs. "Hey."

Gina's breath blew out in a huff along with his name. "Zac..."

He peered at her as she dropped into the chair next to his. "You okay?"

She almost laughed. *He* was asking *her* if she was okay?

"I was just...worried," she said.

"About me?" He sounded amused.

"That does sound silly, doesn't it?"

He was silent for a moment. "It's been a long time since someone worried about me."

"Well..." Her voice faltered. "There are extenuating circumstances..."

"Look," he said. "We both made deals with Sylvester and Carrini to let me stay here. If something happens to me, they'll probably have *both* our heads, so...we should have some ground rules."

"I was about to say the same thing."

"Your house, your rules," he said. "What do you have in mind?"

"Don't go wandering around out here without telling me where you're going," she said.

The amusement came back into his voice. "So you *have* been thinking about this."

"Of course," she said. "What if you were out there somewhere and…"

"And had a dizzy spell?"

"We might never find you," she said. "It's a big place."

He laughed. "It's *huge*! I'd more likely get lost than pass out. I'm a city boy, remember?"

"We'll work on that." She allowed a bit of tease into her voice. "When you're stronger we'll show you our favorite trails. There's one just to the west I walk right from here. But the best ones are in the foothills a short drive away."

He waved his hand toward the east. "What is all the open space out that way?" he said.

"Government land," she said. "Grazing."

He was silent for a moment as if contemplating the possibilities. "So what else?"

"We should set a loose schedule," she said. "I have to spend the daytime hours in the office. I've got a boatload of work to do."

"Anything I can help with?"

She shook her head. "Dale's team had all the film captured by the time I picked you up on Sunday," she said. "I've got to go through it all and figure out what's usable and what's not. What we need to re-shoot and how it impacts the production schedule." She also had copies of the auditions for Sasha's part, but she didn't mention those.

"Not stuff for the actor's eyes, huh?"

"Nope," she said. "Besides, it would be odd to have you there beside me while I'm staring at you on-screen at the same time."

He chuckled. "If you say so. I probably should work on the script anyway."

"You should rest," she said pointedly. "At least for the first week."

He stretched his legs out toward the setting sun. "I feel pretty good right now."

"*Rest* will keep it that way," she said.

"Let me at least take you to lunch," he said. "You do break for food, don't you?"

She laughed. "I'm a fan of food. Especially if I don't have to make it. Most days I'll run over to The Iron Zebra."

"The Iron Zebra?"

"It's a biker bar," she said. "My friend Sabrina owns it."

"So that's it then," he said. "I'll stay out of your hair during the morning and afternoon. I promise this first week I'll stick around the house so you don't have to *worry* about me...and we'll eat. Simple."

"Except for Wednesday," she said.

"What's Wednesday?"

"Dialysis in the morning," she said.

He groaned.

"Which reminds me," she said. "Didn't you say you need more long-sleeve shirts?"

He nodded. "I'd prefer to keep the evidence of...you know... to myself."

"I was thinking I'd run errands while you're at your appointment," she said. "If it's not too personal, I could get you some shirts while I'm out. Unless...you'd like me to go to dialysis with you?"

"Oh, no," he said. "You're already going to miss half a day of work. But I'm a typical guy—not much good at shopping—so the shirts would be great. My size—"

"I know your size," she said before she realized how that sounded. Thank God the sun had set and he couldn't see her blush. "From the, uh, casting info."

chapter 11

The day had not started well.

Zac slept restlessly in the early morning hours, plagued by dreams of Sasha and monster cookies, and he woke with a headache. The kind of headache that reminded him there was poison moving through his bloodstream.

As he listened to the sounds of Christine and Allie getting ready for school, he rolled himself upright and leaned his elbows on his knees, rubbing his head and temples. When the girls had left, he showered and shaved.

He accepted a bagel from Gina but it lay untouched on his lap during the drive to the dialysis clinic. Though he didn't confess to Gina, she surely must have sensed his anxiety. He insisted she drop him at the clinic door, and she did.

He made it to the lobby, where he sat with his head in his hands until a dizzy spell passed.

He met briefly with the director of the dialysis clinic before being turned over to a technician—a peppy wisp of a blonde who did a lot of talking.

It only made his headache worse. He was glad when she left him alone.

He turned on the TV, but the noise made his head hurt. He

tried reading, but the text made his eyes hurt. He wished he'd brought his iPod.

The technician returned, expressing concern about his blood pressure. When the director returned with her, Zac knew it was bad and didn't argue when they suggested he take his prescribed medication; he just wanted them out as soon as possible—and it worked.

He'd never had a problem with anxiety before. Why now?

His phone beeped to tell him he had a text message. He dug it out of his pocket with his unfettered hand.

The message was from Gina: *Earth to Zac. Can U get texts in there?*

For the first time that day, Zac smiled. Carefully he typed: *I read you. What R U doing?*

Gina: *Shopping for your shirts. Which do you like better, green or maroon?*

Zac: *I'm a guy... I don't have a strong opinion. Surprise me.*

Gina: *OK but U asked for it. It's been a long time since I shopped for men's clothes!*

Zac chuckled. *Pretend it's for a production.*

Gina: *That's what wardrobe designers are for!*

Zac: *I'll like whatever U get.*

Gina: *How can U know that?*

Zac: *Because I'm a guy!*

Gina: *Oh, so we're back to that, are we?*

Zac: *What can I say? I only shop for clothes when I have to.*

Gina: *You didn't look good when I dropped you off. Are things OK?*

Zac hesitated. *Better now.*

Gina: *Guess that's good. Hang in there. Gotta sign off…*

Zac: *Over and out.*

Zac set his phone on the tray beside him. For those minutes he'd forgotten his headache.

Until the technician reappeared. "Your blood pressure is much more steady," she said after reading the strip. "The medication must be working."

Zac knew it wasn't the medication; a smile tugged at the corner of his mouth.

*   *   *   *   *   *   *   *   *   *   *   *   *

Zac heard Gina before he saw her. "Can you tell me where to find Zac Davies?"

"You must be his girlfriend." The technician's voice.

Shit. Had she asked about a girlfriend?

There was a pause. "Gina Devereaux." Zac imagined Gina extending her hand. With her hair in a simple ponytail and a light makeup job, she probably struck people as maybe mid-thirties. He, on the other hand, probably looked ten years older right now.

"I'll take you to Zac," the tech said. "In the future you're welcome to find your own way. He'll be assigned to the same machine each time he's here."

"Thank you," Gina said.

"I understand Zac is only with us temporarily."

"That's right." Gina didn't elaborate, and Zac was relieved.

"Too bad for us," the tech said. "We don't usually get younger people in this department."

Their footsteps rounded the corner of the privacy screen.

"Zac, your girlfriend is here."

Gina's eyes narrowed almost imperceptibly on his. But then she slid smoothly onto the bed next to him and ruffled his hair. "Hey Babe," she said. "I brought you a clean shirt."

He took the shirt from her without breaking their gaze. "Thanks."

"How are you feeling?" she said.

Before he could answer, the scrape of a chair pulled their attention to the technician. "We had a little trouble with headaches," she said. "It's not unusual, especially given this was his first time here and anxiety can affect blood pressure, which can cause headaches. We did give him some medication to stabilize his blood pressure, and he should be fine, but take it real easy today—no sudden movements."

When she'd gone, Zac exhaled. "Sorry about that," he said. "The girlfriend thing, I mean."

"It's okay," Gina said. "I was an actor once, too."

"It just seemed easier to let her make assumptions."

"About the blood pressure…" she said.

"So you decided on the green." Zac put his left arm into the shirt sleeve, hoping she'd let him get away with the blatant change of subject.

"Actually, I got both," she said. "Don't you already have medication you're supposed to take for that?" She held the other side of his shirt so he could more easily slip his other arm in. When he didn't answer, she sighed. "Doctor Carrini warned me you wouldn't want to take it. He thought I could persuade you otherwise. Guess I failed in that endeavor. Not that I blame you."

He stood slowly, careful to hold on to the edge of the cart to make sure he regained his equilibrium before he started moving. He wondered what else Gina had discussed with Doctor Carrini. "I say we don't tell him."

He was relieved when she said, "Good idea."

She followed him out the clinic doors—where he came to an abrupt halt. He brought his hand up to shade his eyes but it was too late. His head pounded; he grimaced and reached for his sunglasses.

"How bad is that headache, really?" Gina said as she settled into the driver seat. "Because you don't look real great, to be honest."

"I think it needs more than Tylenol." He was thinking about the Vicodin he still had in his suitcase back at her place.

Gina was silent on the ride, a fact for which Zac was grateful. He leaned into the headrest and closed his eyes. Back at her house, she waited for him to extricate himself from the car. She surprised him by saying, "You do still have that Vicodin, right?"

"I do," he said warily.

"This might be a good time for it."

chapter 12

Zac woke groggy and with the vague impression that his parents had come to him in his dreams again. He sighed and rolled over to check the time. He was amazed to find he'd slept for almost three hours. The girls would be home from school soon.

Slowly he drew himself to a sitting position. The new shirts on the dresser reminded him of the morning's events. Doctor Carrini had said dialysis would get better, but he was beginning to doubt that. He'd been as disoriented and shaky today as he'd been the first time…

And, of course, he'd had no appetite for lunch. In fact, he had yet to make good on his promise to buy Gina lunch, since she'd insisted on leftovers the day before.

He padded into the kitchen. He heard the low murmur of voices and knew Gina was reviewing footage again. He wondered what she saw when she watched him as the character of Aaron Bricewick.

He had just poured himself a glass of juice when the door to Gina's office flew open as if she'd been listening for him.

"You're finally up!" she said.

"Alive and kicking."

"You hungry?" she asked. "I could make you toast, or a

sandwich if your stomach has settled."

"A sandwich would be great," he said. "But I can get it, Gina."

She moved to the counter and waved him off. "Mayo, mustard, or other?"

"Mayo." He leaned against the wall and watched as she pulled bread, meat, cheese, onion, lettuce and mayonnaise from the refrigerator.

"The girls have youth group tonight," she said. "I usually ride with my motorcycle club but..."

"You should still do that," he said. "I'm sure I'll be fine for—what?—a couple hours?"

She nodded. "One of the other parents brings them home. They're usually here by themselves for an hour or so. It'll be kind of nice knowing you're here. Are you sure that would be okay?"

"Of course."

She spread the mayonnaise on the bread.

"So you really meant it when you said you were a biker chick," he said.

She chuckled. "You'll see the proof tonight when the moto girls arrive."

"Moto girls?"

"Willow and Sabrina," Gina said. "We're tight. Like you and your friend Mack." She flashed him a smile. "Lady riders gotta stick together."

He was trying to visualize three women on motorcycles roaring down the street as she placed the sandwich on a plate and handed it to him, then poured herself a glass of iced tea. "It's so nice out," she said. "Let's take this onto the deck."

They settled onto a bench seat. Zac studied the low mountain range in the distance as he chewed on his sandwich.

"I'm making a casserole for dinner," Gina said. "So save some room."

"Do you like to cook?" he said.

"Not particularly," she said. "But when I'm gone a lot, I try to be a 'regular mom' and have sit-down dinners when I'm home."

He took a sip of his juice. "My family always did that, too."

She glanced at him. "Your mom liked to cook?"

"My dad, actually." A pang of regret sliced through him, but he ignored it. "I learned a few things from him. I'll make you dinner sometime. I'm actually pretty good at it when I have someone to cook for."

She smiled at him. "I would like that."

He smiled back, then turned his attention to the low range of mountains. The warm afternoon sun bathed the top edges and made the majestic blue and green hues of the valleys shimmer.

"My mom—" He stopped as a sharp pain pierced across his chest. This was not the poison pain; this was something entirely different.

Gina turned toward him.

He swallowed his sandwich bite with difficulty. "My mom would have loved this view."

He set the last quarter of his sandwich down, no longer hungry. He felt Gina's gaze on him but kept his eyes on the mountains.

"Zac?"

He snapped out of it. "Sorry."

"I don't really know anything, you know," Gina said. "About your parents. None of us does. Just some bare facts."

He cleared his throat. "It's not really something I talk about."

"I understand," she said. "But I wish you could."

He risked a glance at her. She had been staring out at the

mountains, too, but turned her head to meet his gaze. Her voice was so soft he almost missed it. "I wish you *would.*"

After a moment of silence in which he lost himself in her chocolate eyes, she pointed to his plate. "I'll take that in. I've got a few more things I need to get done before the girls get home."

*   *   *   *   *   *   *   *   *   *   *   *   *

Zac was checking email when he heard what sounded like an entire armada of motorcycles.

"Girls!" He heard Gina's voice. "They're here! Are you ready?"

Zac set the laptop aside and stood to look out the front window. Four big motorcycles were pulling into Gina's driveway.

He turned to see Gina enter the living room and nearly did a double-take. She wore a tight shirt with a rhinestone Eagle pattern stretched across her chest. Leather chaps clung to her hips and a leather jacket hung from her hand. Even her hair was in a leather sheath. It was so different from how she appeared on set that he might not have recognized her if he hadn't been in her house.

A slender woman with smooth mocha skin and a long braid down her back walked up Gina's steps and pushed through the door without knocking. "Yo Girlfriend!"

"Willow!" Gina slapped hands with the rider, then hugged her.

"I'm jazzed we get to ride together," the woman said as she released Gina. "I thought you'd be in the City this week." Then she noticed Zac and her eyes widened.

"Sabrina told you about my houseguest, right?"

"Yeah, I guess she did," the rider said. "Looks like a surfer."

"That's because he is," Gina said. "Willow, meet Zac. Zac, this is Willamina. If you ignore her bad manners"—she poked Willow in the ribs—"she's a great gal."

"Yeah, yeah, I'm the cat's meow." Willow shook Zac's hand. "Nice to meet you. I'd stay and chat but the road's a-calling. Are the girls ready?"

"Ready as ever." Christine stood behind Zac, a motorcycle helmet in her hand. Allie, standing next to her, already had her helmet on.

Christine and Allie are going to ride?

"That's my girls," Willow said.

"You sure you'll be okay?" Gina said as the others headed out.

"Of course," he said. "No big deal. Have a good time."

She surprised him by giving him a quick hug. "Thanks. See you in a few hours."

Zac watched as Gina greeted the other leather-clad riders with high fives and one-handed hugs, then threw her leg over her bike. Allie climbed on behind Gina and Christine hopped on behind one of the other riders like she'd done it a hundred times.

Within minutes the street was quiet again.

Damn. Gina was not at all what he'd expected. Her life off the set was full and vibrant...and he was just a temporary interloper. He tried to ignore the unaccustomed sting of envy...

chapter 13

Gina pulled into the school parking lot. She had finished her errands early—the girls' pep rally wasn't over yet—so she sat in the car and let her mind wander.

She started thinking about production issues and the footage reviews she had to finish yet that evening. Instead her thoughts drifted to Zac.

Wednesday's dialysis session obviously hadn't gone well, although Zac had voiced no complaint. She tried not to worry, but there were times she sensed something immense and sad in him. Like when he'd mentioned his mom the other day. She thought he might share something more, but instead he'd clammed up. What had happened to him when his parents died?

He'd seemed better on Thursday; she'd taken him to The Iron Zebra for lunch, where he'd met more of her biker friends. Sabrina, the bar owner and Gina's best friend, even hung out with them for a while. He seemed rather amused with what he called Gina's "biker chick persona."

Gina sighed. Today Zac had insisted—again—that she drop him at the door of the clinic. What was dialysis like for him? Sometimes she felt like she should offer to go with him, but it seemed a bit too…forward. They didn't really know each other that well.

What kind of shape would he be in when she picked him up today?

The next thing she knew, her car doors were being yanked open and two breathless girls were piling in. She was surprised that she'd dozed off, and even more surprised to find it was later than she'd expected.

"Mom!" Allie slammed the car door. "We need to get Zac."

"Well, hello to you too," she said. "And how was your day?"

"Good," Allie said. "But we need to get Zac from dialysis."

Gina recalled hearing part of a conversation between Zac and the girls…what had he told them?

"I'll take you girls home, and then I'll go pick him up," Gina said.

"Mom, you have to take us with you," Christine said.

"I don't think that's a good idea, Christine."

"But we promised," Christine said.

"You *promised*?" Gina looked at her older daughter in the rearview mirror.

When Christine nodded, Gina turned in her seat. "I don't think it was appropriate to promise something that you don't know you can do."

"But mom," Christine said. "He seemed so…"

"So… what?" Gina said.

"So lonely," Christine said. "He doesn't have any family or friends here, except us, and he has to do this dialysis thing a bunch of times…"

Gina looked at Allie, who was also looking more serious than usual. Then she looked at the clock again. "Okay," she said. "On one condition. You two are to stay in the waiting room—at least until I see what things are like for him. Deal?"

"Deal!"

*   *   *   *   *   *   *   *   *   *   *   *   *

"Where is he, mom?" Allie asks.

"He's down that aisle, at the end on the left," Gina said. "But I need you girls to wait here."

She peeked into the room that served as a waiting area. But when she looked back, Allie was already halfway down the aisle, with Christine right behind her. "Girls!"

"Zac!" Allie skidded to a halt.

Gina rounded the corner to see Zac's head snap up in surprise.

Allie gave a frightened squeak and stopped short of Zac's bed, her eyes big as saucers as she stared at the tubes attached to his arm. Christine gasped.

"Girls!" Gina said. "I asked you to stay in the waiting room!"

"It's okay," Zac said. He held his good hand out to Allie, who hesitantly took it and let him pull her toward him. "It doesn't hurt."

Christine stared at his face. "Then why do you look so pale?"

He looked a bit sheepish. "Well, having blood moving in and out of you does create sort of a weird sensation."

"That's so much blood," Allie whispered.

Gina thought Zac went a shade paler at that.

"You're not dizzy, are you?" Christine said.

"No, I'm not dizzy, nurse Christine." He smiled, then waved his hand toward the foot of his bed. "Come on."

She sat without a word. Nobody said anything for several beats. Finally Zac said, "So, do I hear that you girls disobeyed your mom?"

Both girls looked down. He chucked his hand under Allie's chin. "Well, I might be able to put in a good word with her... this time."

Allie beamed at him. He, in turn, looked up at Gina and smiled. She was struck by how handsome he was, even here, in a clinic bed, not feeling all that great. All Gina could manage was to mutter, "Oh, all right."

*   *   *   *   *   *   *   *   *   *   *   *   *

The girls did wait patiently in the outer room while the technician removed the catheters from Zac's arm. But they stuck close to his side as they walked to the car.

"I read that dialysis can make you really weak," Christine said. "Are you, Zac?"

Gina looked up sharply. "And when would you have read about dialysis?"

Christine looked at her shoes. "During study period."

"You used your study hall to surf the Internet?" Gina said.

"It was for an educational purpose, mom," Christine objected. "I'd never heard of it until this morning and I wanted to know about it. I don't have much homework."

Gina opened her mouth, thinking she'd say something about invading Zac's privacy. Instead she met his eyes over the hood of the car, offering a silent apology.

"Well," Zac said, and she had to admire him—again—for jumping in. "I don't feel too bad. But how about you girls take me home?"

"Oh!" Gina said. "Of course!"

The girls spent the ride home talking about their soccer game on Saturday. "You will come, won't you, Zac?" Allie said. "That is, if you're feeling okay?"

"Sure, I'll come," he said. "I'm fine."

Gina parked the car in the driveway, and the girls positioned themselves on either side of Zac as they walked to the house. "I also read that you probably won't have an appetite immediately after dialysis," Christine said. "And that you might be sick to your stomach."

"So Christine and I are going to take care of you," Allie said.

"I thought you girls had plans with Emily and Sarah tonight," Gina said.

"We can see them any time," Christine said. "Zac is only here for a couple weeks."

"And besides, he needs us," Allie said.

"I guess if two beautiful ladies want to take care of me, I should let them." Zac caught Gina's eye and winked. Something in Gina's chest constricted.

The girls sat Zac down on the couch in the living room. Christine went to the hall closet and returned with a blanket. "It also said that you could be easily chilled." Allie took the blanket and laid it over Zac. Gina was reminded of the way the girls used to take care of their stuffed animals: rocking them, tucking them in at night...when had they grown up so much?

chapter 14

Red. Twenty shades of it.

Slosh. Splash…red against a porthole as if he were looking in.

Sharp smell…coppery.

Open mouth, no sound. Echoes… "Mom!"

Window shatters.

Bitter taste, tongue on fire…

Twist. Can't see…can't find …Turn…

Slash!

Zac's own strangled cry brought him to consciousness. He struggled to a sitting position, breathing heavily, bathed in his own blood.

He slapped a hand to his throat.

Not blood…sweat. Just sweat.

A wave of dizziness rolled over him, and he tamped down the urge to vomit.

He leaned forward, holding his head in his hands, willing himself to take deep, even breaths.

A dream. It was just a dream.

He fumbled for the cord that would open the window blinds. Moonlight spilled across the bed, and he dropped to his knees on the floor, resting his forehead against the window pane. But it wasn't enough; he needed air.

He slipped into gym pants and sandals. Carrying a button-up shirt and taking care not to make any noise, he let himself out of the room, through the house and onto the back deck.

The night was cool, and he shivered and pulled the shirt over his shoulders. The moon was only half its full state and cloud cover obscured part of the sky. He sank into a deck chair.

His parents… he hadn't thought so much about them in years. What was it about this place? It wasn't the *emptiness*; that was a feeling he'd long ago gotten used to—and assumed he'd always feel. He just felt…*sad*. And he wasn't sure what to do with that emotion.

He stared out at the mountains, which were just a dark smudge in the night. "I miss you," he whispered.

A slight breeze stirred as if in answer, making Zac huddle into the chair, tucking his feet under him.

A sudden, terrible sound pierced the night, jolting Zac out of a doze. For a moment he thought he was dreaming again…but no, that sound was real…a high-pitched keening that rose in volume and anguish, then stopped abruptly. Whatever it was, it was close by.

And not of this world.

He was already on his feet when Gina banged out the back door and ran past him.

"Gina!" He grabbed the flashlight from its holder on the corner and followed her, his heart threatening to push his throat out of his mouth. He had a moment of vertigo, but his fear for Gina quickly overcame it. How could she run *toward* that awful sound?

He caught up to her at the chicken coop. He went to grab her arm, but something in her hands glinted coldly. A pitchfork.

"Coyote got a chicken," she said. "Nothing else sounds like that."

Holy shit, she was going to battle a coyote with a pitchfork!?

"Point the light over there," she said.

Zac did as he was told. "But the coyote…"

"It's gone," she said. "Here." She handed him the pitchfork and took the flashlight from him. He watched as she used the light to scan the bushes behind the coop, then point it at the ground and circle the area.

She was wearing a light robe, and now and then when the light bounced off the wall of the chicken coop just right he could see the curves of her breast, her hips, her legs. *What did she sleep in?* he wondered.

"Coyote get a chicken, mom?" Christine said. Zac hadn't even heard the girls, but they were standing right behind him.

"I'm afraid so," Gina said.

"Which one?" Allie said.

There was a pause, and then Gina's subdued voice. "The speckled one."

For the first time, Zac became aware of the sound of an ATV. It was close—and fast. He turned as the driver hit the brake, spewing rock as he came to a skidding stop.

"Dirk!" Allie said.

"Girls. Gina." The man on the ATV looked to be about eighty. "You all right here?"

"Coyote got a chicken," Christine said.

"I figgered." His gaze fell on Zac. "Who the hell are you?"

"Be nice, Dirk," Gina said. "He's a guest."

"Oh! You must be the young feller who got pois'nin." Dirk slid off the ATV seat. "And here I thought Gina'd gone done and got herself a new boyfriend."

"Jesus, Dirk," Gina muttered.

"Well, it'd be about time," Dirk said.

Zac stuck his hand out. "Zac Davies."

"Dirk Payne's the name." Dirk's handshake was crushing. "So how you feelin'?"

"Getting better every day," Zac said.

"Guess the little lady doesn't need me checkin' in on her long as you're around, eh, Zac?"

Zac could just about imagine Gina's eyeballs rolling. But her voice came from near the coop, sweet as syrup. "Sure I do, Dirk."

Dirk winked at Zac. "She's one of them independent types."

"Get out of here, you old coot." Gina's voice was teasing.

Dirk climbed back on his ATV. "And none too appreciative, either."

"I'll appreciate it when you catch the coyote *before* he takes my chickens!"

"Yes ma'am." The old man was practically beaming, and Zac couldn't help grinning back at him.

"You girls get some sleep now, you hear?" Dirk nodded at Christine and Allie as he fired up the ATV.

Zac's heartbeat had finally returned to normal by the time Gina got the girls back to bed and joined him in the living room.

"That happen often?" He tried to gauge her mood but it was too dark to read her eyes.

"Couple times a year." She sank into a nearby chair.

"Maybe you need a gun."

"By the time you hear that sound, it's too late," Gina said. "Gun would be no use. It would only pose a danger to everyone in the house."

"I noticed Dirk was packing a big one."

"Well, that's Dirk," she said. "He thinks this is still the Old West."

"And that you're the little lady who needs protection," he smirked.

"It's strange," she said, "but I kind of like knowing he'd be there if I really did need something. Everyone needs someone watching their back, don't you think?"

"Hmm," he said noncommittally. She had her biker friends, her family… and Dirk. All watching her back.

Who is watching mine?

chapter 15

"Christine! Allie!" Gina called as she walked down the hallway. "Do you want to—"

"Shh, mom!" It was Christine's whisper, but it was coming from Zac's room.

Zac's room? When had the "spare room" become "Zac's room"?

She poked her head in. Allie leaned against Zac's bed, a book in her hands. Christine was sprawled on her stomach on his bed, her math textbook open in front of her. Zac lay on his side facing the book, his good arm tucked under his head, fast asleep. Zac had apparently been helping Christine with her homework. *Bless his heart.*

They'd probably worn him out with the soccer tournament and farmer's market—not to mention the interrupted sleep last night. Had it been too much for him?

Gina entered the room and sat on the edge of the bed as she lightly tousled Allie's hair. "I guess we wore him out."

"He *is* getting better, isn't he, mom?"

Gina was surprised by the worry in her younger daughter's face; she knew Zac had done his best to make light of his treatment when the girls were around. "Definitely," she said. "I think being here is helping him heal." She reached over and squeezed

Christine's hand. "Would you girls like to go for a walk?"

"We should wait for Zac," Allie said. "He would want to go."

Allie looked at Zac, so Gina did too. They were all watching him as he stretched and opened one eye.

"What is this?" His voice was scratchy from sleep but the teasing tone came through. "A let's-watch-Zac-sleep party?"

He grabbed Christine and she squealed in surprise. Allie pounced on him, and the three of them rolled around, the girls shrieking as Zac tickled them. Gina was briefly concerned about Zac's arm, but when he grabbed her his grip was strong and sure. He pulled her into the melee.

Several minutes later they all lay breathless and tangled together. Gina stared at the ceiling, Zac's arm resting lightly across her waist, his hand still holding onto Allie's ankle. She turned her head to look at him and he grinned at her. He released Allie's ankle and rolled onto his back. He was so close Gina could feel the heat of his body seeping into hers.

After a few moments of silence, he said, "So what was that about a walk?"

Surprised, she propped herself up on her elbow. "You weren't asleep?"

"Oh, I was." He tucked his arm behind his head, and she noticed he wasn't wearing a bandage on his neck. The stitches were already disintegrating and only a faint line remained as evidence of the catheter. She had a sudden, unexpected urge to kiss him there. *What the—??*

"But I still registered that. It's a special skill I have." His lips quirked.

When she didn't answer he said, "So would this be that trail you told me about earlier this week? Because I'd like to know where it is. I need to start walking every day or I'll get out of shape. And I don't want to get lost while doing it." The quirk turned into a smile.

"Mom, let's go past the Yankee Farm and feed the horses an apple." Christine was stacking her books.

Gina realized she'd been staring at Zac and hastily backed off the bed. "Are you sure you're up to it?"

"Now that I've gotten my beauty rest I am."

*　　*　　*　　*　　*　　*　　*　　*　　*　　*　　*　　*　　*

There was a lot of giggling going on in the kitchen. Gina had tried not to think about Zac and dizzy spells and sharp knives; she didn't want to discourage him from his mission of making dinner. She knew he wanted to contribute and feel worthwhile. But she drew the line at his suggestion that he fix her garage, since it involved him on a roof.

Gina entered the kitchen and burst out laughing. The girls had insisted Zac wear an apron, and they were both jockeying to tie the back of it, even as he tried to cut vegetables at the counter. With his hair a little spiked, and the apron catywampus, he looked... well...adorable.

He threw a towel at her, and the room erupted in more laughter.

When they finally sat down to Zac's masterpiece, as they'd all started to refer to the meal, Gina had to admit it had been a remarkable day. Zac was funny with the girls and good with the townspeople. She'd been a little concerned about what their tight-knit community might make of him, but he had charmed everyone they encountered at the soccer games and the farmers market. Hell, he had the entire town wrapped around his pinky!

Well, Gina, he is an actor, after all.

"So?" he said. "What's the verdict?"

"Huh?" she said.

"The food," he said.

The girls gave their enthusiastic approval, but Zac was looking at Gina, obviously waiting for her response. Interested in her opinion. She picked up her wine glass and swirled it, smiling slowly, drawing out the suspense just a little. "I'm impressed," she finally said.

After dinner, Gina and her wine glass settled on the deck to watch the sunset. The girls had actually volunteered to do the dishes—that had to be Zac's influence, as well—and he soon joined her on the deck, a glass of wine in hand. She refused to be concerned about him drinking wine; it was his choice, and it was not her job to mother him.

"Seems everyone we saw today already knew who I was," Zac said.

"It's a small town." Gina wouldn't tell him how carefully she had laid the story of his presence in their home. Other than Dirk's comment—and that was just Dirk's personality—no one seemed to harbor any illusions that she and Zac were anything more than friends. "Pretty gossipy, too."

"Apparently."

"No more so than L.A.," Gina said.

"You have a point there."

"And I like it better here."

Zac chuckled softly, sending a warm feeling down her spine. "Country girl!"

"S'mores time!" Allie shouted as she banged through the door, a box of graham crackers and marshmallows in her hands.

"Oooh, s'mores." Zac licked his lips. "I haven't had those in a very long time."

"Mom, start the fire!" Allie said.

"Yes ma'am, princess Allie." Gina stood and opened a storage bin, extracting a firestarter log, lighter and lighter fluid. She handed Zac several toasting sticks.

"Can we invite Emily and Sarah over?" Christine said.

"Sure." Gina said. "But you might want to have them bring extra supplies if we don't have a lot."

"I'll tell them." Christine and Allie disappeared into the house, and Zac followed Gina to the fire pit at the back of the yard.

There was a small stack of wood next to the pit and several chairs scattered around it. Gina laid a firestarter log in the center, then built a small tent out of wood. She fumbled with the lighter fluid.

"Here, let me help with that. I've made my share of beach fires." Zac took the bottle out of Gina's hands. "You're going to start yourself on fire."

"I suck at bonfires," she said.

He laughed. "How is it that a city boy makes a better fire than a country girl?"

She shrugged. "You can't be good at everything."

He had the fire going in minutes. He sat back on his haunches, his brilliant eyes lit up by the flames. "Seems you're good at a lot of things, Gina Devereaux."

Caught off guard, Gina didn't have a comeback.

Zac turned his attention back to the fire. "In fact, you're nothing like I thought you were," he mused softly. "So different from how you are on set."

"You too," she said before she could think better of it.

Those eyes came back to hers again, mesmerizing her with their depths. He said nothing, as if an invisible magnet held them together.

The spell was broken by the excited yips of four teenage girls.

chapter 16

Zac was surprised to find he was the last one up that Sunday, considering how late they'd let the fire go.

"That coffee smells heavenly," he said.

"Made it just for you." Gina handed him a mug.

"Mmm. Tastes as good as it smells."

"Come to church with us, Zac!" Allie dropped into a chair next to Zac.

"Oh, I don't know about that," Zac said as he set his coffee mug down. "I'm not much of a church person."

"Why not?" Christine said. "Don't you believe in God?"

"I believe in God, just not necessarily in church."

"You'd like our church," Allie said. "Really."

"What kind of church do you go to?" Zac said. "A little white country church?"

"No," Allie giggled.

"I'd say it's medium size," Gina said from across the kitchen.

"And it's got a stage and a rock band," Christine put in.

"A rock band?" Zac said. "Really?"

Allie nodded.

"The sermons are pretty good, too," Gina said.

"Please Zac," Allie said.

He found himself nodding. Why did he find it so hard to say no to these girls?

*   *   *   *   *   *   *   *   *   *   *   *   *

The church sanctuary looked more like an auditorium. The music was fine—in fact, the music was great—but he couldn't help but think even more about his parents in this place. How many hundreds of times had he sat with his parents in church?

It's just one hour, he told himself.

And he just about made it through that hour. The pastor had just announced the final song when he felt the sensation over his eyes that preceeded a dizzy spell.

Not now.

But once started, there was no stopping it. His hands gripped the chair in front of him.

He shouldn't have come. The idea of God was no longer part of his life.

The black spots formed and bunched together and he knew he risked making a fool of himself if he passed out. Hoping not to draw too much attention from the people around them, he slowly lowered his body to the chair. He rested his arms on the chair in front of him and lowered his head to them, reminding himself to breathe deep and even.

He felt Gina's hand on his shoulder. He placed his own hand over hers briefly and nodded to the question he knew she was silently asking. Her hand didn't leave; instead, it gripped his shoulder more tightly.

*   *   *   *   *   *   *   *   *   *   *   *   *

Gina glanced at Zac. "You're awfully quiet."

The whole car was quiet, the girls reading in the back seat.

"I was thinking about my grandparents," he said.

"Any particular reason?" She said.

He didn't answer for a moment. "They lived four hours away, so we'd go for the whole weekend. It was like a special sleepover."

"Grandpa died of a heart attack in his sleep when I was eight," he continued. "Grandma said it was the best way to go. Shortly after that she got cancer and went to live with Aunt Trudy in Florida."

"Florida is a long way from L.A.," Gina said.

Zac nodded. "The next time I saw her was at her funeral."

"Did you miss them?" Gina said.

"Sure I missed them," he said. "But not nearly as much as…"

Gina glanced at him again; he was staring out the passenger window.

"Your parents?" she prompted, hoping he'd say something about them.

He just nodded, seeming lost in thought, and she didn't press the subject.

He'd seemed so young when she'd first auditioned him for *True Surrender*. She didn't think that way anymore…

"Zac, can I ask you something?" Christine's voice interrupted Gina's thoughts.

Zac turned in his seat.

"It's about this boy. Cody." Christine's face flushed. "I like him but I don't know if he likes me…"

"You want *my* advice about teenage boys?"

"You *were* fifteen once," Christine said.

"When I was fifteen, I was..." Zac's voice trailed off as his face clouded and his eyes grew distant.

"You were what?" Christine leaned forward, the seat belt taut across her budding breasts.

"I wasn't all that interested in girls," he said. "And, besides, I was an ugly kid."

"No you weren't," Allie said.

"That's not possible," Christine said. "You're...you know..."

"You're a movie star," Allie jumped in. "A heartthrob."

He crooked one eyebrow, which only made him more attractive. "I was ugly, honest to God."

"You're not helping." Gina saw Christine's eyes roll in the rearview mirror.

Zac chuckled at her tone. Then he sobered. "Christine, you are an amazing young woman. If a boy doesn't like you for who you are, don't waste your time on him. And for heaven's sake, don't change yourself on his account."

Gina wanted to hug him.

"But how do I know if he likes me?" Christine said.

"Does he tease you?"

"Yes."

"Does he take your books or other stuff and try to get you to reach for them?"

"Yes."

"Then he likes you but doesn't know how to show it," Zac said.

Christine sat back against the seat. "That's pretty much the same thing mom said."

Zac glanced at Gina. "Well, your mom's pretty smart, you know."

"I suppose." Christine sighed, and Gina had to suppress a chuckle.

"The real question is, do you like him enough to take a chance?" Zac said.

Christine suddenly got very bashful. "I want to ask him to the Sadie Hawkins dance."

"Ah," he said. "When is that?"

"In three weeks," she said. "What if I ask him and he says no? I'll be a laughingstock."

"What if you ask him and he says yes?" Zac said. "You could have the time of your life."

chapter 17

The house was oddly quiet on Monday morning once the girls left for school and Gina closed herself in her office. After an hour or so of checking email and surfing the Internet, Zac wandered out to the shed to see what kind of tools Gina had. He thought he might try his hand at fixing that faucet she'd mentioned. The screen door, too. And, of course, the chicken coop. A man had to contribute, after all.

He was sidetracked by the motorcycle.

It was parked squarely in the center of the shed—the place of honor. He circled it, noticing the Harley emblem on the side and the stylized mirrors and floorboards. It was an unusual pale-blue iridescent color with a gray-black wave motif painted onto the tank. The custom paint job suited Gina. In fact, now that he knew her better and had seen her interacting with her biker friends, the whole biker thing was…well, kind of sexy on her.

He stepped around the bike and started rummaging in the various drawers that lined the back of the shed. In short order he discovered he'd need some parts and tools.

He needed a trip into town.

When it got to be noon and all was still quiet behind Gina's door, Zac couldn't stand it any longer. He knocked. No response.

Probably reviewing footage again.

He rapped on her door, harder this time. Then he turned the knob and pushed.

Gina was parked in front of her computer, headphones on, so engrossed in what she was watching that she didn't even hear Zac enter. He noticed himself and Lydia on her computer screen; it was the physical therapy scene.

He placed a hand on Gina's shoulder and she nearly jumped out of her chair. She yanked the headphones off. "You scared the crap out of me!"

"Sorry." His eyes wandered back toward the screen.

Gina hit a button on her computer, freezing the characters in mid-sentence. "Oh, no, you don't. No watching this."

"Why?" he said.

"I don't want any of this coloring what you perceive."

He rolled his eyes. "I need to get some parts at the hardware store. Besides, it's noon. Take a break for food, Director."

Gina glanced at the clock over her desk. "Wow, you're right. I didn't realize how late it was. There's a hardware store a couple blocks from The Iron Zebra."

"Why don't I hit it while we're waiting on our food?"

"Sounds like a plan." She started closing out of her computer programs.

Zac noticed a fat binder sitting on the table behind Gina's desk. It looked suspiciously like…

He picked it up.

It was. And it had Gina's name on it.

He held it up. "What is this?"

"That?" Gina glanced at him. "That is a film script."

"I can see that," he said. "You wrote this?"

She nodded.

"I didn't know you wrote," he said. The woman could act and direct…and write too? He wondered if it was any good…

"Well, you see a lot of scripts as a director," she said. "Maybe not as many as an actor, but a lot. Haven't you ever wondered if you could do it?"

"No," he laughed. "I suck at writing."

"I've got several manuscripts," she said. "That's the only one that's complete, though."

"Have you submitted this anywhere?" he said.

She shook her head.

"Why not?"

"Just never got around to it," she said, suddenly busy studying the shut-down messages on her computer screen.

"But this has to be hundreds of hours of work."

She shrugged. "It helps my directing."

"May I read it?"

She turned back to him, something flashing in her eyes. *Wariness.*

What would Gina be wary of? She couldn't be afraid of rejection…could she? It was such a foreign concept to Zac; after all, an actor's life was all about rejection…

"I need something to do during dialysis," he said.

Still she hesitated.

"Please?"

She sighed. "Okay."

*   *   *   *   *   *   *   *   *   *   *   *   *

Gina clicked off her computer. The house was dark and silent at this time of night. She thought about dinner… about her manuscript.

She picked it up. It was heavy. Solid. Substantial.

And she'd let Zac read it.

She had never let *anyone* in the film industry read her scripts. It was too risky, exposing that dream. What had she been thinking?

Zac said it was good.

It didn't matter.

He wanted to ask questions, talk about it. But she'd clammed up. Why? Because she was afraid he'd see that the script represented something much deeper to her?

What would it be like to see her own words brought to life? Why not submit it, like he suggested? She knew people; he knew a lot more people. And he'd offered. *He'd offered!*

She'd turned him down, and without explanation. She hadn't missed the slight hurt in his eyes. But she couldn't tell him the true reason she didn't want to submit the script to someone else: she wanted to direct it. She wanted to create it, mold it. It was her baby, and she wanted to give it birth.

Geez, that sounded hokey!

It was a dream that was out of reach, anyway. Her work as a director paid reasonably well, but only when she was on a project. And producing a movie…holy hell, that took a lot of money. And she'd be damned before she'd pimp herself or her manuscript out to a money person like Sylvester or Jed.

Jed.

They'd talked about producing their own movie, when they were young and invincible and naïve. Bitterness rose into her throat. Even after all these years, the memories could still paralyze her.

Would that *ever* change?

chapter 18

Zac had managed to fix both the screen door and the faucet in the past couple days, despite the fact that he was only somewhat handy. Now it was time to tackle the chicken coop.

He was digging through drawers of sandpaper and thinking about Gina's script.

He'd read the entire thing at dialysis Monday evening… and it was good. Damn good. Yet when he'd brought it up to Gina, she had *pooh-poohed* it, refused to talk about submitting it anywhere, and changed the subject. What was up with that?

As he bent to pick up a hammer he'd knocked off a shelf, he heard what sounded like a helicopter. He didn't think much of it, but when it got so loud it sounded like it was directly overhead, he stepped out of the shed.

He gawked as the helicopter dipped just behind the house. Surely the pilot wasn't going to land here! He hot-footed it to the deck, where Gina already stood, one hand shading her eyes. She didn't look the least surprised.

"What the hell?" he shouted above the noise.

She turned as if just noticing him there. "It's Sylvester."

It took a moment for that to sink in. "Sylvester? He flies a helicopter?"

She nodded. "He hates traffic."

And he's rich enough to own a chopper.

"But he never comes here," she shouted above the noise. "I get summoned there instead. He must be feeling guilty."

Zac gaped as the helicopter set down right in Gina's backyard. The blades were still spinning when Sylvester jumped out. "Gina!" He practically bounded up the steps of the deck and took her hands in his. Then he turned to Zac.

"Zac." He offered his hand and Zac took it. "How are you feeling?"

"I'm on the mend."

"Good man," Sylvester said. "Things are going well here then?"

Zac nodded and stole a glance at Gina. Had she known he was coming? She could have warned him…

But that was apparently it for niceties. "I'll show you what I'm thinking for the production schedule," Gina said as she turned toward the house.

"And we have to decide what we're going to do about a certain secondary character," Sylvester said.

"Sasha?" Zac swallowed. "She's off the project?"

"Of course she's off," Sylvester said. "At the least, she sabotaged the production. At the worst, she tried to kill you. Her career is over. And I'd say there's a very good chance she'll go to jail."

"Syl," Gina interrupted. "I've got it covered." She stepped through the doorway, and Sylvester followed.

Zac wandered back into the shed, but now he was distracted. What were Gina and Sylvester discussing? What were they saying about him? What were they going to do about Sasha's part?

Sasha.

Gina hadn't mentioned her once.

Sasha was home, presumably. Free to do whatever she wanted.

He gave himself a mental shake. He had a chicken coop to sand.

Sanding didn't require much concentration. In fact, it gave him too much time to think.

Sure, Sasha was off the film...but *she* didn't get needles poked into her three times a week to drain her blood.

He sanded harder.

She had tried to kill him, there was no doubt in his mind, yet she was free. Some bullshit about it being his word against hers... wasn't it his lawyer's job to find proof? Push her to confess? What about the cookies? Didn't they prove what she'd done? What about the eyewitness?

Abruptly he stopped sanding. What *about* the eyewitness? It was someone on the cast or crew...but who? He could find out...

He finished the sanding at a much slower pace. He'd need to get a coat of paint on the coop when it was cooler. Idly he wondered if he'd have enough energy after dialysis.

He got a can of iced tea from the refrigerator and wandered back to the deck. What was taking Gina and Sylvester so long?

Should he ask Gina about the eyewitness? Did he really want to know? What would he do with the knowledge? He couldn't change what had happened... and he liked how comfortable things were between him and Gina. What if she thought it was his fault, for leading Sasha on?

Is that what I did?

He heard Sylvester's voice in the hallway. "I'll have Gerri make the offer today."

Sylvester stepped onto the deck. The two men eyed each other. Finally Sylvester spoke. "I understand you're going to need some additional dialysis sessions."

"That's right."

"Give Gerri a call; she can 'convince' the clinic to schedule your sessions when they'll impact production the least," Sylvester said. "The schedule is pretty damn tight."

Zac nodded. "I'd like to keep the dialysis thing private, if it's all the same to you. The rest of the cast doesn't need to know."

Sylvester looked at him for a long moment before he finally said, "Agreed." He walked to the chopper and tossed his briefcase into the passenger side. "And Zac," he called. "You don't look too bad for a guy who was poisoned!"

Zac and Gina watched the chopper until it was well in the distance.

"Who is the eyewitness?" Zac said.

"What?"

"The eyewitness." He turned to her. "The person who saw Sasha with the cookies."

"Zac…"

"You told me you searched my room on a tip from someone else."

She looked at him. "Are you sure you want to get into this now?"

Suddenly he wasn't sure he did. What if Gina *was* the eyewitness? But he said, "If not now, then when?"

Her brown eyes bored into his. "You realize that's confidential information, don't you?"

"Don't I have the right to know?"

She sighed. "If you ever hope to bring charges against Sasha, you will need this person. And for their own safety, they need to stay anonymous."

For the first time, he was struck by the realization that if Sasha was capable of poisoning him, she might be capable of hurting other people too.

What if she went after Gina?

He suddenly felt cold. He tossed the can into the recycle bin at the edge of the deck. "This is bullshit," he muttered.

"You got that right." Suddenly Gina pushed out a breath. "I need to go for a ride."

The change of topic threw him. She was already stepping through the doorway when he put two and two together. "On the motorcycle?"

She didn't answer. She headed toward the hallway closet where she kept her helmet and riding gear.

"I'll go with you," he said.

She turned just as she reached the closet. "You would want to ride, um…on the back?"

"Don't they call that riding bitch?"

She looked embarrassed and he actually smiled. "Sure, I can be your bitch."

She stopped in mid-reach. "Are you sure? Guys don't usually…"

"Hey, I'm bored and I've never ridden a bike like that," he said. "Besides, I don't give a shit about that macho crap."

"Um…" She rummaged in the closet, pulling out a jacket and a steel blue helmet. "I don't know if I've got a helmet that'll fit you… and what about your dizzy spells?"

"Haven't had one all week." It wasn't entirely true, but they'd been low-key. "Besides, how hard could it be to hold on to you?"

"Holding on isn't the problem," she said wryly. "You're a tall guy; you could take the bike down if you suddenly lean hard to one side."

"So you're saying you can't handle a larger passenger?" His voice took on a teasing tone.

She narrowed her eyes at him, her hands on her hips. "Don't think I don't know what you're doing."

"Come on, Gina," he said.

She appraised his attire coolly. "All right. I'm going to change my clothes. I suggest you do the same. I'll meet you in the shed."

He made quick work of exchanging his ratty work clothes for clean jeans, t-shirt, and the green overshirt she'd bought him. She appeared in the shed moments later wearing jeans and a tank top with a short leather vest over it. Around her waist was a belt made of sparkly stones. She handed him the blue helmet she'd pulled from the closet. "Try this on."

He was about to joke that real bikers don't wear helmets. But as she sat down to put her riding boots on, he forgot his smart-ass comment. Damn, there was something sexy about that image...

He watched through the helmet opening as she pulled her jeans down over the top of the boots and stood. She grabbed the sides of his helmet and shook. "Kind of tight, but better than too loose," she said as she crossed to a high cabinet and pulled out a gray helmet. "It'll have to do. I can wear one of the girls'."

She pulled the gray helmet on. "So you've never ridden a cruiser? Like, ever?"

"I live in L.A., remember?" he said.

"City boy." She grinned.

"Pishaw!"

She threw her leg over the bike, and he couldn't help glancing at the boots again. "So the rules are simple," she said. "Don't get on or off before I tell you I'm ready. No squirming. And most important, lean *with* the bike into the corners, not away. Let the *feel* of the bike and the road be your guide."

He gave a mock salute.

In response, she hit the start button and the engine came to life. She twisted the throttle and a deep, throaty roar filled the shed; there was something primal in how the vibration settled in the pit of his stomach.

She grinned at him as she walked the bike out. She checked her mirrors and flipped the passenger footrests down. "Okay!" she called.

He placed one hand on her shoulder as he swung his leg over the bike. He found the footrests and settled himself into the passenger seat. He looked up to find her watching him in the rearview mirror. She surprised him by grabbing one of his hands and placing it on her waist. "This is so I *know* you're not going to get dizzy and fall off!" she called.

For a moment he was flustered. But she was grinning like a Cheshire cat, and it was contagious. He placed his other hand on her waist and grinned back.

"Ready?" she yelled.

"Ready!"

He had been on yachts and sailboats and scooters. But this was altogether different. The wind rushed by and took his frustrations and worries with it. The vibration of the motorcycle worked its way up his spine like an invisible masseuse. By the time they entered the canyons, he thought he couldn't enjoy himself any more than he already was.

He was wrong. Gina downshifted as they moved into the first of many twisty roads, and he began to understand what she'd said about leaning with the bike and feeling the road. He couldn't help it; he threw one hand into the air and yipped like a young kid on his first rollercoaster ride.

He felt Gina's laughter through her jeans. He caught her eye in the mirror and winked.

*　　*　　*　　*　　*　　*　　*　　*　　*　　*　　*　　*　　*

Near as Zac could tell, they'd ridden a little over an hour before pulling into a small deli on one of the many twisty roads. "I'm starving!" Gina said as she cut the engine.

As he dismounted, Zac was surprised to find he was famished. He opened his mouth to say so, but the sight of Gina tossing her hair from under the helmet was a distraction, and what came out of his mouth was, "Wow."

"I take it you enjoyed the ride?"

Ride? Oh, yes, what a ride that would be...

Zac shook an inner finger at himself; what was he thinking? He just nodded. "Let me buy lunch."

The deli was sparsely populated; they settled into a booth and made short work of placing an order.

"I don't know why Sylvester does this film thing," Gina said. "I don't think he even enjoys it anymore. Maybe it's just an expectation now."

"Or maybe he doesn't have anything else to do," Zac said.

"He used to enjoy making a film," Gina said. "When his wife died, something changed for him."

"When did she die?"

Gina tilted her head. "Five years ago now, I think. Cancer."

"Did you know her?"

She nodded. "I think she's probably what kept him human."

"You argue with him a lot?"

"We have plenty of disagreements," she said. "Just not usually in front of the cast and crew."

"I heard you ordered him off the set."

"I've done that once or twice," she said evasively.

"I mean that day," he said. "The day I passed out."

She hesitated; probably wondering who had told him. "Yes, I did."

"You stuck up for me."

"I did what was right," she said. "I would have done the same for anyone."

"But you believed me about the alcohol and drugs."

"I took your word for it, yes," she said.

"Why?"

"I'd worked with you for several weeks—long days, stressful conditions," she said. "I had a sense of you. I'm a pretty good judge of character when I've spent that kind of time with someone."

It was Zac's turn to go quiet.

"So what is dialysis like, really?" She said. "Does it hurt?"

"A little," he admitted. "The worst part is being stuck there for so long." He paused. "And what I told your girls is true, at least for me. I get this weird sensation…not exactly lightheaded, but like it. They say that will go away with time…"

After a moment she prompted him. "Time?"

He sighed. "This is a long-term thing, I know that. It's just…I can't imagine it in my regular life."

"Does it make you angry?"

"Not angry so much as…" Again he struggled to explain a complex emotion.

"Sad?"

"Why do you say that?"

"I don't know," she said. "I sense it in you sometimes. And even though I'm a grown woman, I still want my mom around when I'm hurt or sick. It's not like you can have that."

Zac was stunned into silence. Did she know how much he'd been dwelling on his parents?

"I think about it a lot," she continued. "Your parents, I mean. Christine being the same age you were…what if something happened to me? They've already lost their father in many ways. He's more like an occasional playmate than a dad."

Zac was glad for the opportunity to focus on a different subject.

"So, what happened—to your marriage, I mean—if you don't mind me asking."

"It's a boring, age-old story." Her eyes took on a tired look. "I thought love was forever. He thought it was only until the next best thing came along."

"You're saying he…" Zac hesitated. "He cheated on you?"

Zac was surprised by the wave of outrage that washed over him when she nodded.

"I thought we would be the exception to the rule." Her voice held a vulnerability and hurt that he'd never heard before. "I thought we could show them all by staying together. I thought… well, I thought there was such a thing as true love, and I'd found it."

Her voice turned sarcastic. "Boy, was I naïve. In the years since he's 'fallen in love' three more times. I've come to realize that we don't understand the concept of 'love' in the same way."

Why did her story feel so real to him? Plenty of his friends had been through similar experiences…

"Would you like to come?" he said. "To dialysis?"

Davies, what are you thinking?

She didn't respond right away; just stared at him. Uncomfortable, he shifted his gaze out the window.

She did the same. "You know," she said, "If we take the twisty roads we won't make it home in time to turn around and get to the clinic."

"I'd like to ride as long as possible."

"Sounds like you're hooked." She turned her attention back to him.

"Out there you don't think about any of your shit," he said.

She smiled. "Now you understand why I keep the bike."

"Do I ever."

"If your appointment was just a little later, we'd have time to ride up to Red Wing Reservoir," she said. "Great roads."

Zac had his phone out before she finished. Two minutes later he'd finagled an extra hour before his appointment.

Twenty minutes later they were back on the bike. Zac rested his hands lightly on Gina's hips as he leaned back, letting the wind take those worries…

chapter 19

When the technician brushed Zac's arm with a dark liquid, he understood the unspoken question in Gina's eyes. "Lidocaine," he said. "It numbs the skin so the needles don't hurt as much."

"Does it work?"

"Some," he said.

He studied her as she watched that first needle insertion. He was determined not to flinch.

But she did…and her features flooded with a mix of emotions he couldn't identify. He caught her hand in his as she started to pull away.

She met his eyes, and he recognized at least one emotion, because he'd felt it so often himself: anguish. But something else: it was as if she was looking into the depths of him. *To see what is really there?*

For the first time in his life, he didn't shy away. He held her gaze as that second fiery needle slipped into his vein. Held it and watched something flicker in her eyes and knew that he hadn't succeeded in hiding the needle's effect on him. But he felt no misgivings about allowing her to see that small vulnerability.

"Zac…" It was only a whisper, but it held so much more. She tilted her head toward him as if to share a secret. He did the same, as if to receive that secret. She was so close he could smell her—a mixture of soap and baby oil.

He desperately wished his left arm was free, because his one and only instinct was to run that hand up into her hair and pull her closer.

Gina's breath was like a feather against the side of his face, and it sent a shiver down his neck.

He sensed the technician testing the access lines, taping the tubing into place, and working with the machine, but he felt suspended…unwilling to move until Gina did.

Only when the tech had left did Gina speak. "I'm so sorry, Zac."

It was not what he'd expected, and it took an effort to keep his voice soft but firm. "You have nothing to be sorry for."

"If I hadn't thought it was the flu… if I hadn't pushed you that day... " Gina began to pull away.

"Whoa, hey." He brought his left hand to cover their hands.

Gina looked down at his arm—at the tape and the tubes and the blood. "If I'd taken you to the hospital sooner…"

"Gina, stop." She could not really think this…could she? "You've got it all wrong."

He breathed deeply. "If you hadn't stood up to Sylvester…if you hadn't taken me to the hospital…if you hadn't figured out what happened… I would be…" He faltered on the word. "Well… you'd be looking for a new leading man."

"I thought the whole thing was completely crazy," Gina said. "I mean, what kind of person…" She shook her head. "I had never seen someone as sick as you were. I was grasping at straws because that's all I could do."

"You saved my *life*, Gina," he said. "And because you found those cookies, I might have a chance at not having to do *this* the rest of my life." He held up his tubed arm. "And if that weren't

126

enough, you invited me into your home when you hardly knew me. Not to mention driving me to these appointments..." He stopped as a disconcerting thought popped into his head. "I hope you didn't do that because you felt guilty."

"No," she said. "I did it because it was the right thing to do."

He could read in her eyes that she meant it. "There is blame, and I suppose I'm going to have to deal with that sooner or later," he said, "but it's most certainly not on you, Gina."

"What *are* you going to do?" she said. "About Sasha, I mean."

"I haven't thought about it," he said.

She didn't respond—as if she knew that wasn't all.

"I haven't been *able* to think about it." He pushed a breath out. "No, that's not it either... the truth is that I haven't *wanted* to think about it."

She nodded slowly. "That might be a good thing," she said. "You need to concentrate on getting healthy."

"And I need to finish this film," he said. "She can rot in jail until I do."

"Be careful, Zac."

"What do you mean?"

"The anger is going to ambush you at some point," she said. "Extreme, off-the-charts, ranting anger. And you know what? It's completely justified. But if you don't handle it right, it will hurt you, not her."

He stared at her for a long moment before responding. "This is advice from personal experience?" She dipped her head.

"My turn for a question," he said.

"Fair enough."

"Do you believe in love?" He'd been thinking about this since their earlier conversation.

Her face registered surprise. "I'd like to believe it exists," she said. "But the older I get, the more I think it doesn't apply to me. Working in this industry…how many couples do you know who've stayed together?"

She had a point there. But…

"I know it exists," he said.

Her eyebrow arched. "From personal experience?"

"My mom and dad had it," he said. "Of course, I was a kid. I didn't know any different so I didn't appreciate it. But I know it now." He paused. "It would be nice to have that one day."

With the right woman.

chapter 20

Zac bolted upright, brought out of his nightmare by his own voice.

"Zac?"

Disoriented by the hallway light, it took him a moment to recognize the silhouette in the doorway. "Gina?"

Her silhouette came toward him. "I heard you. Are you all right?"

Am I?

It was Friday. He'd been to dialysis. He'd heard from his lawyer...

But all he said was, "It's late."

"Past midnight." She lowered herself to the bed. "I was still up. Are you running a fever?"

She reached out her hand as if to feel his forehead, but he tilted his head away from her. "No."

She let her hand fall. In the silence, his ragged breathing seemed to fill the room. When she spoke, it was so soft he nearly didn't hear her. "You had that same dream in the hospital."

He stared at her in the dark. How could she know that? What words had he said aloud? "I ... I don't remember that."

"Will you tell me about your parents?" It was such a simple request, delivered in that same near-whisper, but it caused a torrent of pain to crash through his chest. He opened his mouth to speak but he couldn't. The need to *feel*—a touch, a caress, an embrace—was too strong.

He gripped her wrist and pulled her down alongside him. Without letting go, he brought his arm around her and pulled her tight against his side. She made no resistance, as if she sensed his need. He loosened his hold on her wrist but did not let go. Could not let go, as if it were an anchor keeping him from falling apart.

She placed her hand against his chest and laid her head on his shoulder.

*   *   *   *   *   *   *   *   *   *   *   *   *

Gina lay still, feeling Zac's chest rise and fall erratically, as if every breath bordered on a complete breakdown. Feeling the tension in his hand covering hers. But she was also very aware of the way his body felt against hers, lean and strong.

When she was certain he wasn't going to speak, wasn't going to tell her anything at all, his voice came out of the dark. "It was my second school play," he said. "We were in final rehearsals. My parents were so excited to come and see it…"

He paused, as if gathering strength to continue the story. "I was out late. Later than I should have been. I was thinking about excuses as Mack pulled onto my street and we saw the flashing lights. We didn't realize it was my house until we were nearly at the driveway."

He stopped, and Gina held her breath, silently willing him to continue.

"They wouldn't let me in the house," he said. "I kept asking 'where's mom?', 'where's dad?'… I remember this cop kept saying 'you don't want to see this'… and I *knew*… I knew it was bad…"

"I was only fifteen," he said. "The files were closed. All I knew was that they were beaten to death… and my world as I knew it was over."

His voice became hesitant, shaky. "The day I turned eighteen, I got that file. I was so sure I would find answers in it…"

Gina willed herself to stay still.

"There were no answers," he said. "But there were pictures. I should never have looked at those pictures!" His voice cracked and his chest heaved. "I can't get them out of my head!"

"Zac…" She was going to raise her head but his arm moved and his hand pressed to her head to prevent her from doing so.

"Their hands and feet were tied." His voice was full of anguish.

Gina felt sick to her stomach as she realized that he now *had* to finish this awful story.

"Their throats were slit. It is almost certain my mother was r—" His voice broke. The last word came out a near-whisper and with obvious difficulty. "Raped."

He was silent, but his body trembled, and Gina waited with a sense of horror.

"It was so long ago and I've worked so hard to forget," he said. "Being here with you and your girls, it reminds me… the family dinners, going to church together…Christine the same age I was…" He made a choked sound. "How can it still hurt so much after all these years?"

He released his grip on her head and brought his hand up to cover his eyes. She shifted up so that her face was near his. "It's okay to miss them, Zac. Even now."

She touched his face.

And then his hand was in her hair, pulling her lips to his, and she nearly gasped at the sensation that snaked directly from her lips to her stomach. He rolled her over, pinning one wrist above her head. He hovered over her momentarily, his eyes dark with a mix of anguish and desire. He slid one knee between her legs as he brought his mouth down on hers. The sensation in the pit of her stomach intensified.

He was wearing only boxer shorts, leaving very little to the imagination—nothing to prevent her from feeling his arousal as his weight pressed her into the bed.

He released her wrist and ran his hand down her arm, brushed against her breast and continued down her side to her waist, where his thumb caressed the hollow just above her hip bone.

Without thought, her hands clasped around his neck, finding their way into the hair at the back of his neck.

But his kiss held a desperation, a need to forget, and even as a fire spread from her stomach to her groin, she knew she'd have to stop this. He didn't need sex from her; he could get that from any woman he wanted. He needed something deeper, stronger. Did she have what he needed?

"Zac…"

He broke their kiss and dipped his head to her neck. "God, I'm sorry, Gina."

"It's not that." She was breathless. "It's just…your parents…"

She felt him inhale shakily. Gently he rolled their bodies. Her hands were still entwined in his hair.

"Tell me they're okay, Gina." His words were muffled into her neck.

Gina prayed she'd have the right words for him. "You said your parents loved God."

"Yes."

"Then, Zac, there is no doubt about where they are, and there is no pain for them." She hesitated. "Now it's about you."

"Me? I turned my back on God the day I turned eighteen and got that file." He rolled away from her, onto his back. "How could a loving God let that happen?"

"You have every right to ask that question, and I don't have the answer," she said. "But I do know that Satan is very powerful. He couldn't get your parents eternally, but he's got you. Satan will do whatever he can to keep you from knowing God."

Zac sighed. "Why would God want me now?"

"Oh, He wants you," she said. "He has a plan for you. He wants you to let him into your heart more than anything. Only then can he start to heal it."

"You really believe that?"

"It's happened to me," she said.

"I don't know, Gina," he said. "I don't know if I can forgive Him for what happened to my parents."

"I understand," she said. "But I pray you find a way, because it is only hurting you."

He shook his head wearily, reaching for her and pulling her against his chest. As his breathing evened and slowed, she relaxed into his warmth…

chapter 21

Gina woke, disoriented to find a body crawling into bed with her. She had left Zac in the early morning hours…hadn't she?

"Mom." The murmured voice brought her back to reality.

"Allie, honey?"

Allie's smaller body snuggled up to hers. "I had a weird dream."

Gina felt as though the night had been a dream, too. When she'd left Zac for her own bed, her body had come alive of its own accord, on fire remembering his kisses and the feel of his body against hers. How long had it been since she'd been with a man? Far too long…

"What was your dream about?"

"It was about Zac," Allie said. "He was in a room full of fire."

Fire? Suddenly Gina was wide awake. "What happened?"

"You were there, and Christine and me… all trying to put water on the fire to put it out," Allie said. "And then I woke up."

Gina swallowed. Was Allie's dream a coincidence?

"Mom!" Now Christine was sitting on her bed, too. "Guess what Zac is doing?"

"What?"

"He's making breakfast burritos!"

"Ugh," Gina said. "You like breakfast burritos?"

"I don't know but I'm going to find out!" Christine was up and out the door again.

Gina looked at Allie. "Well…what do you think?"

"I think Zac is nice," Allie said. "I wish he could stay."

Gina felt the same way…and she couldn't afford to. *It's probably a good thing we go back to the set tomorrow.*

The thought depressed her.

*   *   *   *   *   *   *   *   *   *   *   *

"Anyone else up for a canyon hike?" Zac said over breakfast burritos.

The girls were all for it. Gina felt sluggish and wished she could get away on the motorcycle for a few hours. *Some fresh air and exercise will probably do me good*, she thought.

So she agreed.

Apparently Zac was fully recovered, because he pushed ahead, strong and purposeful. Gina found herself bringing up the rear. The closeness she'd felt with Zac the night before was gone, leaving only a vague ache for that connection with another human being. A familiar loneliness settled over her.

When they reached their favorite swimming hole, Zac stripped off his shirt and cannon-balled into the water. He cajoled Christine and Allie into the cold water and proceeded to splash them and chase them around until they teamed up to try to dunk him.

Gina sat on a rock and watched. He certainly didn't act sick. And then it struck her: *He's not sick. He doesn't need me anymore.* For some reason that thought made her feel even more inconsequential… like she'd felt when her girls hit certain landmarks and no longer needed their mommy the same way.

Finally he pleaded exhaustion and pulled himself up on a rock near her. Gina did her best to ignore his wet, naked torso and the still-vivid memory of the night before. The girls tried to talk him into jumping from the higher ledges. To Gina's relief, he didn't join in, but he did plenty of cat-calling and jeering as the girls climbed up to jump into the pool over and over again.

Was she being overly sensitive, or was Zac actually *ignoring* her? What was different about him this morning?

It struck her half-way back to the car. He wasn't ignoring her; he was *acting*.

She should have picked up on it sooner; after all, she'd watched him for hundreds of hours on the set and on-screen.

But why? Why would he feel the need to *act* with her? It was fake, and something fake with Zac felt all wrong after the night before. Unless he felt like the night was a big mistake…

By the time they reached the car she was pissed.

How dare he try to pull that with me!

*   *   *   *   *   *   *   *   *   *   *   *   *

As the girls headed for their rooms to change their clothes, Zac stopped in the kitchen for another cup of coffee. He glanced up from the mug and was surprised to find a layer of iciness in Gina's eyes.

"What?" he said.

"Do you know how many minutes of footage we've shot?" she said.

She was talking about the film, he realized. "It's got to be thousands."

She nodded. "And I've watched every minute over again. Some ten times. Some a hundred. I've studied you for *hours*. I know when you're acting. And you've been doing it all morning. Why?"

137

His acting ability had gotten him out of more situations with women than he cared to think about—starting with his Aunt Trudy. He had never met a woman who could tell when he was "on"—hell, sometimes he didn't even realize it himself, it was so automatic—and it was downright uncomfortable that Gina could.

"Is this about last night?" she said.

Last night...

"No." Last night had been both awful and wonderful...and he owed it to her to be honest about it. But what if he himself couldn't identify all the emotions of that time? "Yes."

She cocked her head. "You showed that you are a human being with vulnerabilities. So now you feel the need to prove that you're a tough he-man?"

"It's not like that," he said. "I just don't know how to..."

She stood with her hands on her hips.

He tried again. "I've never told anyone that stuff about my parents."

He face softened. "Zac, what happened last night was intensely personal. I would never tell anyone else."

"I know you wouldn't," he said. And it was true, he realized; she was a rare person in the world he inhabited, with her morals and faith and respect. "But it's more than that. It's..." He'd healed in more ways than one over the last two weeks, but he didn't know how to tell her that.

And how to explain the kisses, which he didn't understand himself?

"I don't know if I can explain what it's meant to me," he said. "That you let me stay here. I love how *real* it is here."

I love how real you are when you're here.

"Then please just be real with me," she said. "No games. Not now, not here. I have enough fake relationships in my life."

He heard the emotion in her voice but didn't know how to respond.

She took a deep breath. "We only have one more day," she said. "When we get back on set, our relationship has to change. *We* have to change."

"I know," he said. "But we have tonight. I can't begin to repay you for what you've done, but I want to do something for you. I want to take you to the biker party."

"I do want to go to the party," she said. "And with the girls at their friend's house…"

Zac heard the hesitation, but also sensed her desire. "Everything has been pretty heavy since I came here. I think it's time we had a little fun, don't you? Besides, I want to show you a good time; you deserve it."

She shrugged.

"I understand how it is between us and I'm fine with it," he said. "Why don't you think of it as a date with no expectations? Just a chance to relax and enjoy yourself while someone else deals with the details. I'll even drive you home if you want to drink."

Her eyebrow quirked. "You think you're okay to drive?"

"I'm fine."

Finally she smirked. "So, are you going to act the biker dude?"

His brow furrowed, and she laughed.

"Wait," he said. "I have an idea. Christine! Allie!" He moved toward their rooms at the far end of the house. "Girls! I need your help."

"With what?" Christine poked her head out her bedroom door.

"I need to go shopping," he said. "Without your mom."

"Why?" Allie had reached his side now, too.

"I need to become a biker," he said.

"You mean you want to dress like a biker and act like a biker?" Christine said.

"Exactly."

Christine and Allie looked at each other, then smiled. "I think we can be of assistance," Christine said.

chapter 22

Gina parked in a gravel lot. As they neared the field, she suddenly got nervous. What if people thought Zac was an actual date?

What if she wished he was?

"Gina?" Zac turned to her. "You coming?"

She hadn't realized she'd slowed down so much.

"Zac…about us…"

"We've already covered that," he said. "Tonight is about you, and I'll do anything you want. Live a little, Gina. Let yourself have a good time."

She looked at him: the leather chaps over the tight jeans. The vest the girls had picked out for him open at the neck. A curl of hair escaping the bandana around his head. The belt buckle above his well-endowed…

Gina shook her head. *Biker* looked damn good on him.

But she couldn't tell him that.

And she didn't dare let her mind wander to the kisses they'd shared last night.

"I'll be watching out for you." His eyes were hard to read with the sun setting behind him, but the earnest tone in his voice was impossible to miss. "Trust me?"

She smiled; the tables were turned. She held out the car keys. "Just make sure we leave in time to pick up the girls."

He grinned, pocketed the keys, and offered her his arm.

*　*　*　*　*　*　*　*　*　*　*　*　*

Zac had never been to a biker event of any sort, and he watched with wonder as the bikers who'd gone on the charity ride rolled in, engines rumbling like constant thunder, American flags flying.

Gina had told him about The Patriot Riders, a biker organization that focused on all things American. There was a heavy contingent of military and ex-military amongst the riders, and he couldn't help but think of Mack. This seemed like a fitting way to honor him and others like him.

He pulled out his phone and snapped a photo, taking a few moments to attach it to a text message to Mack. Gina peered over his shoulder, then broke into a wide grin when she saw what he was doing.

The line of bikes seemed to stretch forever, gleaming chrome reflecting the setting sun. Gina stood beside him hollering and waving at the riders. They trotted along with the last of the riders, waiting until they were mostly parked before wading into the melee to greet Gina's friends.

Zac had never seen so much leather in one place. He loved the way bikers greeted each other; bear hugs and hip checks were the norm. There were introductions all around; thank God he was good with names.

Most of the riders were camping in the fields next to the stage area, so while they were stowing gear, Zac got Gina a drink and they wandered amongst the bikes. He got a kick out of her "oohing" and "ahhing" as she pointed out features on bikes that he was sure most women would never even be aware of.

When the band started tuning up they wandered toward the stage area. The microphone came to life with announcements and good-natured B.S.

Gina's friends joined them near the stage.

"Hey everybody!" Willow said. "I want you to meet my friend Andie. She's a biker, too."

The petite red-haired woman with Willow did a little wave to the chorus of hellos.

"We grew up together," Willow said. "In fact, we learned to ride together."

"I've been gone for awhile," Andie said.

"Yeah, she got the hell out of dodge," Willow said. "But she's back and she wants to ride."

"You definitely should ride with us," Gina said.

"Thanks," Andie said. "But I don't know how long I'll be in town. I really only came to settle my dad's affairs."

"Sorry to hear that," Gina said, but Andie just shrugged.

"It doesn't matter how long you're here," Sabrina said, jostling the man next to her. "You're welcome to join us *girls* for a ride anytime."

Before Andie could answer, Willow threw herself at Andie and squealed, "It's so cool that you're here!"

Another round of drinks appeared just as the band started to play.

The band, too, had a decidedly patriotic bent, and Zac found himself grateful. Grateful for the freedom that he took for granted. Grateful for the reminder that there were bigger things in life than a film. He was quickly coming to appreciate why Gina chose to be associated with these people.

And the band could *rock*. "Come on!" he shouted to Gina. "Let's dance!"

Even the dancing was different here. When dancers stepped out it wasn't for attention; it was because they were just carried away. Everyone else cheered them on, stomping and clapping along. They were just there to have fun, not to "be seen." They weren't looking for a hook-up like in the clubs in L.A.

He didn't have to be anything more than a guy out showing his girl a good time.

His girl.

Now he was starting to sound like a country boy!

It was true though. The best part of the night was seeing Gina loosen up and have a good time. He took pleasure in being the one who could give her that.

When he tried to take a break from dancing, he was lassoed by Willow and Andie. "Come on, Zac, you owe us one!"

Gina waved him off good-naturedly, so he did a round of dancing with Willow and Andie (and several other women who joined them), all while keeping an eye on Gina. Each time he looked it seemed another man had been pulled into her circle. An unaccustomed feeling caused him to falter momentarily.

Was that *jealousy*?

He shook his head; he had no claim on Gina and this was not a *date* in the usual sense of the word. But the next time he looked, she had another drink in her hand—which man had purchased *that* one for her? —and she was laughing at something one of them had said. That's when he decided it was time to reclaim Gina as his dance partner.

Willow was drifting toward a biker who had apparently caught her eye, and Zac pulled Andie over to the small group. Gina pulled him into the circle and introduced him to "the boys." He made small talk for a while, but as soon as he could, he slipped one arm around Gina and suggested they return to the dance. She slipped her hand into his and let him lead her back into the gyrating bodies.

But they couldn't dance forever; they had to take a break sometime. While Gina visited the ubiquitous portable toilets, Zac wandered off for another drink for Gina (and a pop for himself).

He hadn't quite made it back to Gina's friends when he found himself stopped by two women in skimpy tops and heavy makeup.

"We haven't met," the shorter blonde woman said. "I'm Debra. My friend is Sarah."

"Nice to meet you," he said as he glanced past them.

"I haven't seen you before," the dark-haired one said. "I would definitely have remembered you."

"I'm from out of town," he said. "I'm just visiting friends. Speaking of which…"

"You're delicious," the blonde said. "Why don't you dance with me?"

He held up the extra drink to indicate he was already on a mission. To his surprise, it was lifted from his hand.

"Sorry, ladies." Gina took a sip of the drink, her eyes appraising the two women. Her hand ran down Zac's arm. "He's all mine tonight."

He shrugged at the two women as Gina took his hand and led him into the throng of dancers.

"Nice save," he said as he wrapped his arm around Gina's waist and pulled her into him. He sensed a slight stiffness in her that hadn't been there before.

"Debra," Gina said. "I should have known."

"So she has a reputation?"

"She's actually quite nice when she's not drinking," Gina said. "I think she's just lonely. The other one I don't recognize. Must be a new friend of Debra's."

She pulled back from his embrace and eyed him coolly as

145

she took another sip from her drink. "You seem pleased with yourself," she said.

"What do you mean?"

"Everyone wants to dance with you."

He rolled his eyes, then pulled her toward him again. She made no resistance. "Don't think I haven't noticed a number of the men eying you," he said.

She shook her head slightly. "Eight or ten years ago, maybe…"

"You don't see it, do you?" he said.

"See what?"

"You're selling yourself short, Gina," he said. "You are both sexy *and* smart."

"Well…" She blushed. "I feel that way tonight."

He smiled and wrapped his hand over hers, pressing it tight against his shoulder. "Good," he murmured into her hair.

When she'd had enough of dancing they found their blanket at the far edges of the light, up on the hill. She parked herself between his legs and leaned against him as they watched the dancers below.

He leaned in to speak into her ear. "Are you having a good time?"

"Hmm." Her right arm came up and her hand found its way into the hair at the nape of his neck, creating a pleasant tickling sensation. He tucked his chin into the soft hollow of her neck and inhaled her scent. A sudden image from the night before rose sharply in his mind: Gina on her back, her wrist trapped above her…

"Zachariah," she said, her voice husky. And just like that, his groin tightened. *Was she thinking about the same thing?* "Would you take it the wrong way if I kiss you?"

He was sober, but she wasn't. Was it wrong to feel this attracted to his *director*?

"This night is about you," he said. "Whatever you want…"

"I just mean…without it having to mean something…and nothing more…"

She shifted to sit sideways across his lap, and he felt himself becoming aroused.

"Without it being weird in the morning…" she continued.

His hand came around her hips and all he could think was *God yes, kiss me*.

But she hesitated just short of her mouth on his. A sly smile graced her face as she shifted again, pressing herself into his groin. "I think you would like that, too."

Before he could form a response, she brought her lips to his. Geez, she even *tasted* good; a hint of rum-and-coke and pure female…

He'd always prided himself on his control, but he quickly realized that Gina's fire ran deep. Yes, he was sober, but the smell of her perfume and the feel of the leather smooth against his hands made him *feel* intoxicated.

Careful, Davies.

Gina shifted again, and before Zac knew it she was straddling him, and he was pulling her hard into him, bringing his own urgency into the kiss, his hands running up the smooth leather of Gina's chaps and pressing into the small of her back.

They both came up for air at the same time, breaking the spell. They went still, foreheads resting against each other, trying to catch their breath. "Oh boy," he whispered.

… And Gina *giggled*.

He couldn't help it; he chuckled.

It must have been infectious, because Gina giggled again…and he laughed…and they toppled backward.

chapter 23

Zac's mind was still on Saturday night as they drove to L.A. the next day.

Zac hadn't had that much fun in…well, he didn't think he'd ever had that *kind* of fun.

And Gina…whoa.

He could still see her, swaying suggestively to the music, the stones in her headwrap and on her belt picking up a sparkle from the band's lights, her hair falling loose and soft around her shoulders, stretching out her arm and crooking her finger at him…

Feeling *attracted* to his director was one thing, but last night he'd been on a path to straight-up *desire,* and that was something else entirely…

"In point-six miles, turn left on Haddock Street."

The canned voice of the GPS brought Zac out of his reverie. They were almost to his apartment.

*   *   *   *   *   *   *   *   *   *   *   *   *

"So this is it." Gina set Zac's gym bag on the counter. "The great bachelor pad."

It felt odd to have Gina in his apartment. "Such as it is." It was even more odd to think she wouldn't be right across the hall tonight…

They stood awkwardly.

"So I hope everything goes okay with Doctor Carrini," she said.

"I'm fine," he said. "I'm ready to go back to work. Ready to finish this film."

"Will you do something for me?"

"Anything," he said. "You name it."

"Tell me if…"

"If?" he prompted.

"If you have any dizziness. Any headaches. Even just a general exhaustion." Her voice was insistent. "You have to let me know."

"That's not going to happen—"

"Zachariah." Her voice was stern. "I mean it. And if anyone messes with your schedule, you let me know. You *have* to get to dialysis. No film is worth…" Her voice faltered. "…what you've been through already."

Again he was touched, and when he spoke his voice was quiet. "Okay, Gina."

"Promise me."

"I promise," he said. "Is that what's been bothering you? You were quiet all the way here…"

She sighed. "You're not just an associate or co-worker anymore, Zac. I consider you a friend."

"I feel the same way about you," he said.

To his astonishment, she teared up. "I don't have a lot of friends," she said. "I certainly don't look for friends on the set…"

He disagreed—she had friends where he had acquaintances—but he didn't interrupt.

"And I know I'm going to lose your friendship," she said.

He frowned. "Why would you think that?"

She shrugged. "That's just how it works."

"Because you're directing me?" he said. "That's ridiculous. That's got nothing to do with it. Sure, our relationship has to change, as you've pointed out, but it's only a few weeks, and then…" He stopped at the look on her face. "What?"

"You'll change your mind," she said. "When you see how I am, how I *have* to be to get this job done…"

"Gina." He took her hands in his. "I want this film to be as bang-up awesome as you do. I'll do my part, and you'll do yours. And when it's over, we can be…whatever we want."

"You're right," she said, but he could tell she wasn't convinced. Carefully she extracted her hands. "You're right," she repeated as if trying to convince herself. She stepped to the door, looking over her shoulder as him. "I'll see you in the morning, then."

"I'll be there."

chapter 24

By morning Gina had given herself a stern talking-to and was in full director mode; she had only a few hours until the entire cast and crew showed up. Still, when she saw Zac striding toward her in the late morning, she had to steel herself. He was wearing the green shirt she'd bought for him and sporting a fresh haircut, and he looked for all the world like the movie star he was.

She took him aside privately to ask how his appointment had gone, and was relieved to hear he had the official go-ahead from Doctor Carrini. They talked about how much he wanted the cast and crew to know, as well as how his dialysis was to fit into the schedule.

"I know you're not comfortable having others see your arm," she said, "but we have some scenes—notably the intimate scenes—where we can't very well have you fully dressed. I need to know if we have to re-script positions or camera angles to accommodate."

"You're right," he said.

She looked at her watch. "We've got a little time; let's see if Suzie is back."

Gina knocked on the makeup artist's door.

"Hey Gina," Suzie said when she answered. "Zac, you look good. What's going on?"

"I've got a challenge for you," Gina said. "But I can't give you an explanation and I've also got to ask you to keep this in confidence."

"Of course," Suzie said.

"I need you to take a look at Zac's arm."

"Zac's arm?" Suzie's face registered confusion as her gaze shifted to him.

Gina nodded to Zac. He hesitated, then rolled up his left sleeve, turning the inside of his arm toward Suzie.

"Huh!" It was obvious Suzie wanted to ask...but she didn't. Instead she took his arm in her hands and ran her fingers lightly over the graft. Gina saw Zac flinch, although not from pain, she was sure.

"I need to know if you can do anything," Gina said. "I'd prefer to do the scenes as scripted. If we can't, I need to know now."

"There's only one way to find out," Suzie said.

"Find me in the conference room when you're done," Gina said.

*   *   *   *   *   *   *   *   *   *   *   *   *

Gina was pouring over loglines with Dale when Zac and Suzie entered. "Any luck?"

"It was easy enough to handle coloring," Suzie said. "The bumps, though...not much I can do about those."

Gina knew the "bumps" well enough, but Dale was in charge of lighting and cameras, and would ultimately be responsible for what the camera picked up. "Let Dale get a look."

Again Zac hesitated, but Gina couldn't help that. Dale squinted at Zac's arm. Then he placed a hand on Zac's wrist and moved the arm up, down, and from side to side.

"Well?" Gina finally broke the uncomfortable silence. "You got this handled?"

"Yeah," Dale said. "We can handle this. Just build in some extra time in makeup each day and we'll do the rest."

"So what's the story?" Suzie said.

"The *story* is that Zac got food poisoning." They all jumped at Sylvester's voice. "And I don't even want to hear *that* discussed amongst the cast and crew. We have a job to do, people."

Suzie excused herself quickly. Gina stood with her hands on her hips looking critically at Sylvester.

"What?" he said.

"Nothing." She looked at her watch. "The cast and crew should be gathered in the dining room by now." Without waiting for him, she strode out of the room.

chapter 25

"Cut, cut, cut." Gina frowned.

Zac suppressed a frustrated sigh. It was like he couldn't get in the swing of things...he just wasn't in sync with what Gina wanted. He had his own ideas about the character he played, but Gina didn't seem to want to hear them. It had been that way all week. And worst: Sylvester had been breathing down their necks. It had been a miserable week and he was exhausted.

Gina was talking to him. "I'm getting too much *fear*. You still have your pride, your demand for respect as a military officer. You're not *afraid* of her, you are pissed off that she has seen you vulnerable. Because no one gets to see that side of you."

He had to remind himself she was talking about his character. "So give us *wary* and maybe a little *defensive* instead," she continued.

Gina looked at her watch. "I don't want to shoot this scene again next week." She stepped back behind the camera and circled her finger in the air. "And roll."

*   *   *   *   *   *   *   *   *   *   *   *   *

Zac came awake with a muffled cry, his heart beating hard and fast. He was overly warm even though he had only a bedsheet covering him. He looked at the clock beside his bed: 5:45 a.m. The last time he'd had this nightmare, he'd wakened to find Gina at his side…

He had no explanation for what had happened that night. What he did know was that somehow, something deep inside him had been released. He'd held his share of women, but had never *been held* by a woman.

He sighed. He missed the ranch and the girls. And if he was honest with himself, he missed *that* Gina.

Okay. If he was *really* honest with himself, it was more than that. He was mighty attracted to Gina. How the hell had that happened?

He hadn't left *Director* Gina on good terms. Without invitation, the conversation replayed in his head…

"We're all under pressure," she said.

"Yeah, but that doesn't mean you have to take it out on me." His tone was accusatory.

"Take it out on you?"

"You were all over me," he said. *"And you didn't want to listen to what I had to say."*

She sighed. *"Zac, I have a job to do. And that job includes getting the best performance from each and every actor I direct."*

"I just want equal treatment," he said.

"I don't have the luxury of being exactly equal or fair," she snapped. *"If I'm harder on you it's because I know you're capable of giving me more. It would be the same with any other actor."*

"Damn it." He swung his feet over the side of the bed. He was under pressure, sure. But Gina was probably under more...due to events that *his* situation had brought on. She hadn't complained once. Yet here he was, getting overly sensitive about a few comments.

He had trusted her with his personal secrets, and she had shown herself more than up to that. From a professional standpoint, her track record was solid, but even more to the point, her direction of *him* had been on-point since they'd started the project.

The answer to his frustration was simple, he realized: he needed to let go and trust her on this too.

He reached for his running shoes. Maybe a little fresh air would help him get his head in the game, and when he got back on set later that day, he'd find Gina and set it right.

chapter 26

It was just past eight on Sunday evening when Gina checked into the hotel. She headed for Zac's room and was startled when he stepped out of it just as she rounded the corner.

He looked as surprised as she. "I was just coming to see you," he said.

"Well, since I'm here, can I come in?" she said.

He held the door open, and followed her in.

"How are you?" she said once the door was closed. "Was dialysis okay?"

"It was fine," he said.

"You didn't drive, did you?"

"I drove to the appointment, and Mack drove me home after." He sat down on the bed.

She was relieved to hear that, and she couldn't help thinking about what had happened the last time he'd had dialysis. It had only been a week ago. But that wasn't why she was here…

"Look," she said. "I owe you an apology. I think I *was* harder on you than I should have been."

"No, Gina. You were right to push me." He paused. "You tried to warn me that our relationship would have to change when we got to the set. I didn't believe it. I didn't *want* to believe it." He took a deep breath, as if that realization was still uncomfortable. "Subconsciously or not, I expected different treatment because of our friendship. I over-reacted and took your comments personally. I'm sorry."

Gina blinked. She wondered if this man would have recognized all that a mere three weeks ago…

"But we're both professionals and we both have a job to do," he said. "From here on out, what you say, goes."

Gina looked down at her hands, debating. Finally she said, "There's something I want to tell you."

"Okay."

"But you can't share this with anyone," she said, wondering if it was the right thing to do.

"You know I won't."

She took a deep breath. "I don't want to direct much longer. At least, not in Hollywood."

"But Gina," he said. "You're incredibly good at it. Don't you like it anymore?"

"Thanks." She blushed. "But there are other things that are important… like my girls. I just can't be with my girls enough."

"I want to work one more job," she continued. "I need *True Surrender* to be a blockbuster so I can get a good offer, one that will set me and the girls up so I can pursue… something else."

It took a few moments for that to sink in. "But what will you do instead?"

"Maybe I'll direct school plays." She gave him a somewhat sad smile. "It's a little late, but I need to be a mom. With one more good project, I can finally swing it financially."

"What about your ex?" he said. "Doesn't he have money?"

"Oh, he has money," she said. "Tainted money. I don't want

any more than our alimony agreement entitled me to. Enough to support the girls, that's it."

"What do you mean by tainted?" he said. "Surely you don't mean he's involved in something illegal?"

"It's not like that," she said.

"Well, what is it like?"

She thought about telling him. But he had never been in love (by his own admission); and besides, it was more than that. If she started talking about inner beauty... how Jed's had slowly leaked away... how it had stolen hers too... what would Zac think?

That you are a desperately sad, empty woman, that's what.

So she said, "It's really none of your business."

She saw the hurt in his eyes, but it was quickly covered. "Of course it's not," he said. "We are just... co-workers."

"Associates," she said.

"Right."

chapter 27

The next week went more smoothly. Zac was back in his element, Sylvester had backed off, and Gina was singularly focused on the story they were trying to tell. Even the retake with Sasha's replacement went well.

Gina was packing her suitcase Friday afternoon when Zac tapped on her open door. "Got a little extra room in your suitcase?"

"Why?" she said.

"I got something for the girls." Zac looked sheepish. "Could you take it to them?"

Gina stared at the small shopping bag he held.

"This *is* the weekend of the big Sadie Hawkins dance, isn't it?" he said. "That boy didn't back out on Christine, did he?"

"No, he didn't."

"Good, then I won't have to kick his ass." Zac held the bag out to her. "I bet she'll look amazing. Pretty exciting as a mom, too?"

"Scary." She took the bag somewhat hesitantly. "Do you mind if I peek?"

"I sort of expected you'd want to," he said, then quickly added, "I hope you don't mind."

Gina sat on the bed and opened a box labeled *Christine*. It was a Native American necklace made of turquoise stones.

"She said her dress is aqua blue," Zac said.

"That's right." Gina didn't know what to say; the necklace was a perfect fit for the dress.

"I had a little help from Mack on that one," he said. "And there's something for Allie too."

Gina opened the other box. A silver necklace with a simple horse charm. It was perfect for Allie. How could he have gotten to know them so well in such a short time?

"Tell Allie to keep working on those math problems and I know she'll get them." He glanced at the clock beside her hotel bed. "I'd better get going or I'll be late to dialysis."

She looked up at him; when would he have had time to do this? "Zac, I don't know what to say…"

"Please don't say anything," he said. "I just… I miss them. They're my friends too."

He paused at the door. "You've got great girls, Gina."

*   *   *   *   *   *   *   *   *   *   *   *   *

The gifts were a hit.

In fact, Christine and Allie wouldn't stop talking about Zac. How dreamy he was…how sweet he was…how they missed him. It was starting to get on Gina's nerves, which were still frayed from the long week of shooting.

And then: The Question.

"Mom," Allie said. "Do you think we're ever going to get a stepdad?"

Gina suppressed a sigh. "I suppose if it's meant to be, someday I'll remarry."

Allie flopped onto the couch. "I wish we had one like Zac."

"An actor?" Gina scoffed. "No thank you."

"I don't see what's so bad about actors," Allie grumbled. "Dad is one."

"Yes, he is," Gina said. "And you see how well *that* worked out."

"But mom, Zac isn't like Dad," Allie said.

Gina set her lips in a tight line; they were young and didn't know any better.

"How many times have I told you never to settle for less than what you deserve?" Gina said. "That you can have real love?"

"Lots," Christine said.

"So don't you think I deserve the same?" Gina said.

"Sure, but…" Christine said. "How do you know it when you have it? I mean, you and Zac could have that…"

"Stop it," Gina snapped. Then she felt bad. "Come here, girls."

She waited until they were seated beside her. "Look, we're doing just fine, right?" she said. "Yes, sometimes it would be nice to have a man—a stepdad—around, but I'm not willing to marry someone just for that reason. I want someone who cherishes me. Just like what I want for each of you. Okay?"

"Yeah, mom, we know," Christine said.

Allie gave her a hug. "Love you, mom."

"Love you too." But Gina couldn't help feeling that she'd let them down somehow.

chapter 28

"I'd like to try this shot a little differently," Gina said.

It was after 9pm and they'd already had a long day of shooting. Everyone was either kicking back in their rooms or unwinding in the common area. Everyone but Zac, Lydia and Gina, that is. This romantic scene just would not come together the way Gina wanted, and they were running out of time to get it right.

Zac sighed. It felt like being in detention.

"Zac, instead of Lydia turning toward you before moving into the rest of the scene, let's try having you approach from behind and stopping just short of her, almost but not quite touching," Gina was saying.

She stepped behind Lydia, emulating what she wanted Zac to do. "Long pause. Brush your hand up this arm slowly…draw this out. You almost lost her just when you realized you loved her. We'll put a camera right in your face. Lydia, you're going to startle a bit, then—up and over with your arm."

"Zac—" She moved to him, now playing Lydia's part. "When she startles like that, when her arm comes up and over…" She twisted herself as Lydia would. "I want you to pull her in. She's not going to fight you on this." She pressed against his chest briefly in her demonstration of the embrace, and Zac was caught off guard by the flash of attraction that zipped through his body.

"Then go into the dialogue."

She moved out of his arms. "I want you guys to play with this idea," she said. "See what feels most natural. I'm looking for chemistry here, not script-by-word. Okay?"

He nodded and turned to Lydia. Gina let them go all the way through the scene, calling "cut" just before the kiss. "Something is off." She frowned. "Do you feel it?"

Zac *did* feel it. He and Lydia needed a certain chemistry to do this scene, and it was becoming harder and harder to conjure it up. Why? Were his real-life feelings for Gina getting in the way?

Davies, you're an actor. Create it.

Lydia nodded. "Maybe he's not having to reach far enough to pull me in?" She'd been struggling, too. Earlier in the day she and Gina had had a long heart-to-heart about something…

Zac watched Gina pace in the small conference room they'd commandeered. She did that when she was thinking…or *envisioning*, as she called it. Sometimes she stared at a person without really seeing them, like she was now with Lydia. When she did that on set, the entire cast and crew always fell silent, so he guessed he wasn't the only one who found it fascinating.

And it usually worked.

The shrill tones of a cell phone broke the spell. Lydia jumped. "I need to take that." She bolted to her purse and pulled out her phone. Gina continued to pace until Lydia cried out "Oh no!"

Gina exchanged a glance with Zac.

"I'll get there as soon as I can," Lydia said.

"Your grandmother?" Gina asked. Zac could only surmise that her grandmother had been the topic of conversation earlier in the day.

Lydia nodded. "She doesn't have much time. I'm sorry, but I… I have to go."

Gina helped Lydia put her things in her bag. "We'll see you at 8."

Lydia nodded obediently and ducked out of the room. Gina stood looking after her, obviously still in deep thought.

"What now?" Zac said.

Gina blew her breath out in a huff. "I'll run it with you," she said. "In the morning, you can guide Lydia in what I want. You're the lead on this anyway."

Holy shit, he was going to run this scene with *Gina*?

She took her place opposite him, and he could see her mentally switch into the role.

Well, okay then.

She moved away from him. He followed. Grabbed at her arm. She shook him off. *That wasn't in the script.*

The words he needed came without thought, so he concentrated on the actions and the emotions. He made another attempt at her arm, and this time she stopped but did not turn.

He took one step toward her. Stepped slowly around her until he was in front of her. Waited for her to meet his eyes. (There were supposed to be tears there.) Continued the argument. Pulled her toward him. She resisted, placing her hands flat against his chest. He looked down at her hands, and so did she, surprise on her face.

Surprise at the strong chemistry that flowed between them.

A real reaction?

Slowly she raised her eyes to his. He gathered her into him, and though her hands were still against his chest, she let herself be hauled in.

He forgot he was acting (he *was* acting, wasn't he?). The desire he was supposed to feel for his co-character was suddenly no problem.

In slow motion, Zac lowered his mouth toward hers.

"And cut." Gina's voice was hushed.

"No," Zac whispered. He didn't want to stop there. Gina was no longer the director, no longer the character of Holly. He brought his lips to hers.

Gina went rigid in his arms momentarily—just as her character was supposed to—but then relaxed into him, returning the kiss with just enough pressure, just enough tease, that he couldn't help but part his lips, seeking to taste her, to get her to do the same.

And she did.

He forgot everything except how she tasted, how she smelled, how her hands felt as they slid up and over his shoulders to bury themselves in the hair at the nape of his neck.

He stepped her backward until she was pressed against the wall—which was definitely *not* in the script. The feel of her body pressed full-out against his made him struggle for breath. "Gina..."

"Zac." She broke the kiss. "Stop."

Her hands moved back to where they'd started on his chest. But this time they exerted considerably more pressure. "Stop, Zac."

He nearly stumbled as he took a step back.

What the hell had just happened?

"We can't do this," she said.

"What? Why?"

"You're kidding," she said.

"I don't see one reason why we couldn't."

The look she gave him was both incredulous and irritated. "I guess you wouldn't."

"What is that supposed to mean?" His voice came out more defensive than he'd intended.

She didn't respond; she started packing her notes into her bag.

"You act like a kiss is going to ruin everything," he said.

"It's not the kiss," she said. "It's where the kiss would take us."

"That's pretty presumptuous," he said, hating the sarcasm in his voice but unable to curb it.

She gave him a look that said *give me a break* and he realized that would be a losing argument. He'd known exactly where he wanted to take it from that kiss…and he was peeved that she didn't want him as much as he wanted her.

"Look," she said. "I have a job to do, and so do you. We've got three weeks of shooting to cram into ten days. We can't afford any distractions."

"Speak for yourself," he said. "I could actually use a little stress relief."

She straightened and faced him. Her eyes flashed with anger and something else he couldn't identify. "Well, if that's all it is for you, I'm sure you could run along down to the local bar and find someone else to help you with your *stress relief*."

She hauled her bag onto her shoulder and made for the door.

"I just might do that," he said to her back.

Without looking back, she said, "I'll see you at 8 a.m."

*   *   *   *   *   *   *   *   *   *   *   *   *

Zac *did* end up at the bar.

For a drink.

Which he knew was a load of bull, but being mad was easier to handle than the sting of rejection.

It didn't take long to find what he was looking for. Or rather, it found him. The girl was at the bar buying a drink when he invited her to sit. She was tall and slim. Long blond hair. His type.

Or what used to be his type.

She sat. They flirted. He bought them another round.

They made it to her car before he kissed her. The next thing he knew, she had her hands on his chest, and all he could think of was how Gina's hands had felt in that exact same spot. Smaller. Hotter. He shook his head ever so slightly and concentrated on the girl. On the kiss.

She snaked her hand up under his shirt, and he did the same as he backed her up against her car.

But he imagined a shorter frame. More curves. Fuller breasts...

Abruptly he pulled back.

Shit. Why can't I get into this?

"Zac!"

For a moment he thought the girl had said his name. But no, it came from farther away, from somewhere behind him.

He heard it again. His head jerked to the left and his hands dropped from the blond's side.

"Candy?" he said. "What are you doing here?"

The PA skidded to a stop, looking embarrassed. "I...I didn't know you were busy," she stammered. "I just thought... since you don't go out much...maybe you were with some of the, um... others."

Zac stared at Candy. She was observant and bright, but extremely shy. She had probably said no more than twenty words to him during the entire shoot.

And, unbelievably, he *was* relieved to see her.

"Now that you mention it, I did promise I'd help Wyatt with his lines." Zac turned to the girl. "I'm sorry. I didn't mean to... well, I really should go."

To her credit, the girl didn't go wishy-washy on him. She stood with her hands on her hips. "Whatever." She rolled her eyes, yanked her car door open and got in.

Zac looked at Candy and shrugged.

chapter 29

"Zac, the director wants to see you pronto." The crew member jerked his thumb over his shoulder at the video trailer.

It was a bright day, and Zac pressed his fingers on the lingering heaviness over his eyes. *Might as well get this over with.*

He peered into the trailer. Gina was bent over the desk, and he caught a glimpse of himself on a computer monitor. "You wanted to see me?" he said.

"I did." She straightened as if with effort. "What happened last night after I left?"

"I took your suggestion."

For a moment she looked stricken, but it was quickly covered. "And?"

"I'm sure you're aware of what went down."

Her brow furrowed. Was it possible Candy hadn't told her?

"You *do* know that I was unsuccessful in my quest," he said.

She stared at him for several moments, as if gauging his response for truthfulness. "And how would I know that?"

"Didn't you ask Candy to keep an eye on me?" he said. "To make sure your *asset* did not drink too much… to make sure your *asset* was not damaged?"

Her lips pursed into a flat line and her hands went to her hips. "What the hell, Zac? You ought to know me better than that."

Oh, Gina was mad.

And she had a right to be.

"First of all, you're a grown man and even if I wanted to stop you from making a mistake with some one-night woman, I wouldn't. What the hell do I care?" She glared at him.

"Second, I didn't ask anyone to go snooping around on you. That's insulting. And third," she continued. "*I'm* the one defending your dialysis sessions to Sylvester. *I'm* the one working the schedule around to meet deadlines. If I was Sylvester, I'd feel that gave me the right to monitor your every action. But I'm not, and I won't."

For the first time he noticed the dark circles and fine lines around her eyes. Gina was exhausted.

"So I think you'd best get out before I say something else I might regret."

"Gina…"

"Goddamnit, Zac." She turned away from him. "Just get out. Please." Her shoulders sagged and the fight was out of her voice. All he really wanted to do was go to her, take her in his arms and…why did that feeling keep creeping up on him?

"Out!" She barked.

* * * * * * * * * * * *

Gina didn't emerge from the trailer for a long time. When she did, she had transformed again. There was no trace of the anger or defeat he'd witnessed; just a singleminded focus.

How does she do that?

She spoke to the cast and crew for several minutes, laying out what she expected for the scene as was her morning ritual. As everyone took their places, she pulled Zac aside. "So, back to last night." She spoke low so that only he could hear. "You're still frustrated. Use it. Take that sexual frustration and desire denied and funnel it into this scene."

He stared at her. Perhaps she was a better actor than both Lydia and him. Had the kiss they'd shared last night really meant nothing to her?

"Jesus, Gina," he said. "You think that's all that was?"

Her expression registered confusion, and he wanted to smack himself in the head when he thought about his crack about stress relief.

Then another thought came to him. Could she have engineered the whole thing? Could she have done it on purpose to give him what he needed to nail this scene? He'd already seen her gift for motivation in action…

"You're the lead on this, Zac," she said. "You have to bring the desperation into it. I know you can do it."

She turned from him, calling to one of the other cast members. Despite their altercation, she believed in his ability. And he'd be damned if he would let her down…

*   *   *   *   *   *   *   *   *   *   *   *   *

The crew was busy setting up the next set when Gina and Dale emerged from the video trailer. Cast members were lounging in the shade or sitting in the makeup artists' chairs, waiting for the next scene to be called, but she didn't see Zac amongst them. Despite the rocky start they'd had that morning, he'd done some amazing work, and she wanted him to know it.

"Where is Zac?" she asked one of the gaffers.

He jerked his thumb toward the beach. "He got a phone call and took off."

Zac sat alone on a low fence about fifty yards away. Something about the way he held himself gave her pause. "Give me some time alone with him," she said to Dale.

He nodded, and she knew he'd run interference if need be.

As she came up behind Zac, she noticed he held his head in his hands. *Not a good sign.*

She stopped next to the boulder. Without looking up, he greeted her. "Gina. I was just going to come find you."

His voice sounded hollow. She sat on the rock next to him. "What's up?"

He rubbed his hand across his forehead. "I made you a promise that night we came back."

He didn't elaborate, so she said, "Which is it? Headache? Dizziness?"

"Both."

She breathed in carefully. "Do you have anything with you?"

"I took some Vicodin," he said. "But it shouldn't have happened at all. I haven't had any…well, okay, I've had maybe a few minor waves of dizziness."

"Maybe because you're at the tail end of the dialysis cycle?"

"Maybe." He tossed a pebble. "I only had two beers last night, but I felt much more affected than I should have. Something about the dialysis…or perhaps the poison…" Unconsciously he hugged his left arm to his chest while the other hand covered his graft, and Gina was broadsided by a sudden protective urge.

Zac turned his gaze to her. "The truth is, nothing would have happened last night, even if Candy hadn't shown up."

"Zac, you don't owe me any explanation."

"I know, but…" He winced and rubbed his head again.

"Why don't you lie down in my trailer?" she said. "Just until the headache eases. No one will bother you there. I need to talk to Dale."

And that's where he was, reclining on the cot with a cool cloth draped over his eyes, when she entered the trailer fifteen minutes later. She was rifling through her notes, wondering if they could change the shot sequence, when Zac spoke. "There's something else I should probably tell you."

Her hands stilled on the papers. "Is this something I want to hear?"

His lips twisted in a wry smile. "Sasha called me."

It took a moment for that information to sink in. "*What*?" she demanded. "When?"

"Yesterday morning when I got up there was a message on my voice mail," he said. "She had called sometime in the middle of the night."

"What did she say?"

"Not much coherent," he said. "She was crying, ranting, begging me to give her a chance to explain."

"Holy shit," she breathed. "You didn't call her back, did you?"

He shook his head. "I gave the message to Detective Gray."

"What did he say?"

"He said she's supposed to stay far away from me, and that he'd check into it," he said. "But he just called and said she's missing."

"Missing?"

"They don't know where she is." He massaged his temples.

Gina was silent. How unstable was Sasha at this point? She'd spent a week in jail before getting out on bail…which meant she'd been out for what? Four weeks already? Why contact him now? Was it just a slip? Maybe she'd been drunk?

"I'm sorry, Gina," he said. "This shouldn't be your problem. And I really don't think Sylvester needs to know…if you get my drift."

"But Zac…"

"It's nothing serious," he said. "I just thought you should know."

"Just one more thing you've got to deal with," she muttered.

"Maybe the *frustration* will drive my performance."

She looked at him. "Are you kidding me?"

"Yes, actually, I am."

"Okay, you got me," she said. But she was thinking: *You don't need that kind of 'help'*…

*　*　*　*　*　*　*　*　*　*　*　*　*

The rest of the afternoon passed quickly, and though Zac was obviously tired, he came through. Gina released the cast, and she and Dale took the day's footage into the conference room that served as their darkroom.

They hadn't been there more than twenty minutes when a hotel employee knocked on the door. "Miss Devereaux? You're needed in the manager's office."

"What is it?"

"Apparently some sort of accident with one of your cast."

Zac! She stood so fast she nearly knocked the chair over.

"I'll hold down the fort here," Dale said.

The young man escorted her to the manager's office. She looked from the manager to Zac, who stood at the window with his hands shoved into his pockets. "What's going on?" she demanded. "Zac, are you alright?"

"I'm fine," Zac said.

"It seems we have a breach in security," the manager said, just as Sylvester strode into the room. Detective Gray was right behind him. In his hands was a basket, and in the basket was…

Cookies?

"Are those what I think they are?" Gina said.

"These were found in Mister Davies' room," Detective Gray said. "Apparently someone placed them there while he was out."

There was silence in the room. Gina glanced again at Zac; his eyes met hers ever so briefly before looking down, then out the window. Anywhere but at the cookies, she noticed.

Then Sylvester's voice exploded. "You're telling me someone *broke* into his room? What the hell kind of security is that? Zac is a very important person. We could be dealing with a stalker here!"

"Mister Amos, it's my opinion that this is likely the act of one person," Detective Gray said. "Sasha Stone."

"You haven't found her?" Gina said.

"She's missing!?" Sylvester roared.

"No, but we will, rest assured," the detective said. "Until then you might want a little extra security around this place."

"You're damn right we want extra security!" Sylvester barked. "And *you* people will provide it." He pointed at the detective and the manager.

Detective Gray took a bracing breath. "The two of you can discuss that with my partner in the next room."

Sylvester glared at the detective as he was led out of the room. There was no doubt in Gina's mind that he would harangue the poor manager next.

The detective turned to Gina. "I've asked one of my associates to escort you to your room."

"What?!" Zac suddenly came to life. "Why? You don't think—"

Detective Gray held up his hands. "It's a cautionary measure only, Mister Davies. We believe Miss Stone's ire is focused on you, but she *is* aware of the fact that Miss Devereaux was instrumental in finding the original cookies."

"But she doesn't know the identity of…?" Gina said.

"We don't think so," the detective said.

Another officer entered the room. "Miss Jackson is waiting in the lobby," he said.

"Miss Jackson?" Zac said.

Gina held her breath.

"Who is Miss Jackson?" Zac demanded.

The detective hesitated.

"He has a right to know. " Gina turned to Zac. "Miss Jackson is the eyewitness. Candy."

Zac looked stunned. "The production assistant? Candy is the one who convinced you to search my room?"

Before Gina could respond, Detective Gray broke in. "I need to talk to Mister Davies—alone."

chapter 30

Gina stared at her computer screen. It was no use; her concentration was shot. And if she went down to the video suite she'd have to deal with other people…and at the moment she just couldn't muster the mental energy.

She might as well face facts: she was freaked out. It had never occurred to her that Sasha would target *her*.

She paced her hotel room, feeling like she was in lockdown. There was a guard in the hallway, for crying out loud.

She nearly jumped out of her skin when someone knocked on her door. "Who is it?" she called.

"It's Zac. Can I come in?"

"Zac!" She quickly crossed the room and opened the door.

"Are you all right?" He looked at her, then past her. "There was nothing in your room that shouldn't be?" He moved into the room, scanning it as if he'd be able to tell if anything was amiss. "Nothing missing or damaged?"

She closed the door. "Everything was just as I'd left it."

"You haven't had any hang-up calls?" he said. "Or odd notes?"

She opened her mouth, then closed it. The same questions the officer had asked her. The skin on the back of her neck prickled.

There was something they weren't telling her...

He turned back to her. "Gina?"

"You got a note?" she said.

He looked at his feet.

"You did!" She stared at him. "What did it say?"

He shook his head.

"Zac..." she said sternly.

"No," he said.

"Damn it, Zac, tell me what the note said!"

Without warning, he crushed her to his chest, wrapping his arms around her so tightly she gasped. "If something were to happen to you, Gina...if she did something to you or the girls..."

Gina couldn't answer; all she could do was cling to him.

His voice came as a low raspy whisper. "I think I would kill her."

Gina couldn't help it; she shuddered. Not just at the possibility of bodily harm to her or her children, but because it must be bad to push someone like Zac to even *think* about murder.

After several moments, Zac eased his grip and lowered them both to the edge of the bed. Gina gripped his hands and stared into his eyes. "Please, Zac. The note."

"It's just a crazy woman's rambling."

"I trusted you with the information about the eyewitness," she said. "Now you have to trust me with yours."

He sighed. "Okay, Gina, you win." He hesitated. "It said 'I know where you spent those two weeks and I know you slept with her'."

Gina's stomach dropped. "I'm officially freaked out."

In more ways than one.

He touched her face. "I feel responsible, don't you see that?" he said. "I *need* to protect you, Gina. I'm going to arrange a restraining order for you and the girls."

"But…"

"Will you just let me do this?" he said. "Please?"

She leaned into him, and he put his arms around her again.

After some time, he spoke again. "I have to go." He smiled ruefully as he released Gina and stood. "I need to talk to Candy."

She let him lead her to the door, where they stood, hands still clasped.

"I'm scared for you," she whispered.

"She can't do anything more to me," Zac said.

Gina pushed up onto her toes and planted a light kiss on his cheek.

She felt more than heard the sharp intake of breath. He stared into her eyes for a long moment. "Good night, Gina." He squeezed her hands once, then reached for the doorknob.

"Good night Zachariah."

The door clicked softly behind him.

chapter 31

Gina peeked into Christine's room, then Allie's. God, it was good to be home. She hung her bathrobe on its peg and slipped into her own bed.

What a shitty day. Her heroine was grief-stricken over her grandmother's death, and her hero was being stalked. They still hadn't found Sasha. The entire cast was on edge. And Sylvester didn't help matters by hovering over them all day. It had been all she could do to hold everyone together. Thank God it was Friday.

Friday. Dialysis day. She hadn't had a chance to talk to Zac before he left. She hoped he was okay.

It was getting hard to keep her usual level of professionalism where Zac was concerned. Every time she regained it, he did something to make her lose it. Like the gifts for her girls. Keeping his promise about the dizziness. His obvious concern last night…

And the kiss. She'd purposely kept herself so busy that she fell into bed each night, too exhausted to dwell on it. But she still felt Zac's lips, his mouth…his solid muscle against her chest…

Her body trembled. How long had it been…?

She was home. She didn't need to keep up pretenses. What would it hurt to fantasize a little? She closed her eyes, finally allowing herself to relax…

*   *   *   *   *   *   *   *   *   *   *   *   *

Zac lay in bed, fully wrapped in a blanket. He was chilled and felt sick to his stomach.

Damn dialysis.

Yet he knew it wasn't just that.

Detective Gray had called with the news that Sasha had been found and was in custody. The detective expected bail to be set high enough to keep her there for awhile. That was good news.

And Zac had arranged for the restraining order for Gina and her girls.

Having Sasha reappear in his life—*right now*—was almost more than he could handle. But he would. He would not let Sasha derail him, he vowed. He *would* handle the dialysis. He *would* do the best damn work he could as the character of Aaron Bricewick. He could even handle his feelings for Gina...

Everything that was coiled tight inside him loosened as his thoughts drifted to Gina. Gina on her motorcycle. Gina at the biker party. The surprised look on her face when he pulled her into his arms.

The passion in her kiss.

She was very careful about how she came across to the cast and crew, but that kiss hadn't been an act. She was as attracted as he.

He would play by her rules. And when the shoot was over, and they could be anything they wanted...well, he wanted to see how deep that passion went.

chapter 32

"There's no way we're going to meet this schedule," Sylvester growled. "We need to shoot over the weekend. End of story."

Gina couldn't argue. They had finally gotten the intimate scenes but still had the fight scene, which would take a long time, not to mention the flashback torture scene…

Her first thought was how that would impact Zac's dialysis session. It also put her in a bind with the girls, since her nanny didn't work weekends and her mom and dad were out of town. Complicating the matter was the fact that her girls were off school the next week. Originally they would have wrapped production in time, but now the girls would have to spend the weekend on the set, and the following week with their father…*or with his chauffer or service staff*, she thought sarcastically.

Sylvester had been intolerable all week. He'd stood over her shoulder. He'd barked at the crew. He'd criticized the cast. It had been all she could manage to keep the actors' minds on what they needed to do… and herself too, for that matter.

"I came to the same conclusion," she finally said. "And here's what I think we should do…"

*   *   *   *   *   *   *   *   *   *   *   *   *

Zac had been looking forward to Saturday; even dialysis on Friday didn't dampen his anticipation. He made sure he was in the hotel restaurant at 7:30 a.m.

"Zac!"

He turned in time for Allie to throw herself at him. "Allie! Christine!" Now he had one girl in each arm. "Oh my God, I can't believe you're really here!"

"We can't believe it, either," Christine said. "Mom *never* lets us come on set."

"There's good reason for that," Gina said. "But perhaps you're old enough now."

Zac turned to Gina. "Good morning, Director."

"Good morning, Zachariah."

"Let's sit together!" Allie said, and Gina made no argument.

Once they were seated, Zac said, "So you girls haven't ever seen your mom direct?"

They shook their heads.

"Man, are you in for a treat," he said. "If you watch closely, maybe you can figure out her secret."

"Secret?" Christine asked.

"The secret of how she gets us to do exactly what she wants," he said.

"You work *for* her?" Allie said.

"Well, everyone pretty much works for the director," Zac said. "At least during the actual shoot."

"After that, Mom and Beth spend *weeks* in the video suite," Christine said.

Zac chuckled. "Yeah, that's where the *rest* of the magic happens."

"Okay, girls, time to talk about rules," Gina said.

They groaned.

"The only way I can let you stay is…"

"We know, Mom," Christine said. "This is a workplace."

"Yadda yadda yadda," Allie said.

Zac laughed out loud. "Well, when we're done shooting for the day, can I take my girls out to dinner?" he said.

"Can we, mom, please?" Allie said.

"Including their mother, of course," Zac added.

Gina shrugged. "I'm going to work you so hard today, you'll be too tired to eat."

Was that actually a mischievous glint in her eye?

"Mom!" Christine said.

"Oh, all right!"

*   *   *   *   *   *   *   *   *   *   *   *   *

It had been a magical weekend for Zac…and the girls, he hoped. He'd spent every spare minute with them, showing them the ropes and letting them watch the makeup artists and production crew at work. Saturday dinner was late, and they were all tired, but it didn't matter.

He knew he probably shouldn't get so attached to Christine and Allie, but he couldn't seem to help himself. Besides, he had every intention of keeping them in his life after this shoot was over.

He tucked his arm behind his head.

One week, he thought. *Only six more days, and I can tell Gina how I really feel.*

chapter 33

To Zac's surprise, Gina was drinking at the wrap party. Liberally. But then, so was everyone. There was a lot of hand-slapping and a hilarious "spoofs" video that Dale's camera folks had put together, as well as the "wall of shame" awards and the more serious gestures of appreciation from the cast to the crew.

It was nearly midnight when the party broke up. Many of Zac's compatriots were headed to the bars to continue the celebration. But when Gina headed for the elevator, Zac fell into step beside her.

"Mind if I walk you up?" he said.

"Zachariah." She tucked her arm into his as they stepped into the elevator. "Do you realize that you are going to be famous? *Famous!*"

She was more drunk than he'd thought.

"You're going to be a shtar." She made a big flourish with her free arm. "I know it." She leaned into him, nearly tipping over, speaking soto voce. "And I know theesh things."

"Gina…"

"It's what you've dreamed of." Gina's voice got excited. "It's what you worked so hard for. It's why you didn't die from the poishon!"

"You are going to have your pick of scripts," she continued as they stepped off the elevator on her floor. "You can go anywhere. You can do anything you want!"

"Gina, listen." He stopped them in the hallway. "There's something I've wanted to tell you. Something that has nothing to do with the film."

She cocked her head.

"You remember when I said that after the shoot we could be anything we wanted?" he said.

"Yes," she said. "I remember."

"Well, I want to be more than friends, Gina," he said. "I want to be *with* you."

She didn't say anything. But the way she held herself, head still cocked to one side, the urge to kiss her was overwhelming. He leaned toward her.

"Oh, no, you don't." She laid her hand on his chest, which only made him desire her more. "I might be attracted to you but I'm not having sex with you. I won't cheapen our relationship like that."

"That's not what I'm saying at all," he said, dismayed that she would think that. "That's not what I want."

"Yes it is," she said. "And I'm not holding it against you. I'm flattered. Really. Especially considering I'm quite a bit older than you."

Zac was confused. Why was it that he could have any other woman *but* the one he most desired?

"Look." She started moving down the hallway toward her room. "This is going to be your time, Zac. You think you'll want to hang out at my place? No."

Zac opened his mouth to protest, but she beat him to it.

"We've been living in a *created* world," she said. "Now we have to go back to the real world. In your world, a casual sexual relationship is fine. In my world, it's not."

Then she added under her breath: "Especially not with a famous actor."

Gina had to be the only woman on the planet who would hold that *against* him, he thought.

"I need to go home." She was suddenly very serious. "Home to my daughters." She slipped her card reader into the slot with some difficulty. "Good night, Zac."

She disappeared into the room, leaving him standing in the hallway.

chapter 34

Zac lugged his suitcase into his small apartment. The door closed with a soft *click* in the noon quiet. He stood for a few moments, just looking around without really seeing anything. Gina had left early without saying goodbye. Why did that hurt so much?

It was probably for the better. She was probably right. Maybe he had some late-stage adolescent-type crush on his boss. Maybe it was just lust or desire. (Well, hell, of *course* it was that, but...) Why did he feel so empty?

But the emptiness was nothing new; it had been his constant companion since his parents died. But even with the sadness he'd felt during those weeks he'd spent with Gina and her girls—the night he'd told Gina about his parents would be forever seared into his consciousness—he hadn't felt *empty*. Not like this.

His phone dinged. It was a text message from Mack: *Getting together at Billy's tonight, can you make it?*

How did Mack know he was back already?

He texted back: *maybe.*

Maybe it was just what he needed. Maybe he was reading too much into this empty feeling; maybe it was just the letdown he typically felt at the close of a production.

Mack's response: *Come on, it's Saturday night!*

He had done it. He'd held it together and made the best damn film he could. But he was tired; all he really wanted was be alone.

He sighed. Texted: *I'll be there.*

He would take a nap before he went out, he decided. He left the suitcase where it was.

chapter 35

The thing about having your office in your home is that you constantly feel like you should be working, Gina thought. But no, she was doing her best to take the two days off she'd promised herself.

That's why she and the motorcycle were parked at this scenic overview. She set her helmet on the ground next to her and lay back on the grass, letting the sun soak into her skin.

She was relieved that shooting was over. She couldn't remember ever having to put so much effort into staying focused on the job, the story. It was why she picked scripts she loved—because she *lived* them for so many months.

Was it her age? Was it the constant arguing with Sylvester? Was it all the unusual distractions?

Like Zac…

In her more honest moments, she had to admit that part of her relief was *not* seeing Zac every day. It had gotten increasingly difficult to treat him like the rest of the cast…to treat him the same way she would treat any other actor in that position. Her feelings for him ambushed her at the most inopportune times…

Her lust.

Well, at least I'm still capable of lust, she thought wryly.

She worried about him, too, with the dialysis and all. When would the full import of his situation hit him, and what would he do when it did?

chapter 36

It had been several weeks and Zac's life had taken on a semblance of normalcy. In fact, his thirtieth birthday almost slipped his mind until Mack brought it up. They were out celebrating with friends when his phone indicated an email message from Gina. His heart skipped a beat. He excused himself and found a quiet spot to read the message.

"Hey guys, I'm attaching the movie trailer that will release on Friday. It's amazing! Give yourself a big high-five. BUT! You HAVE to keep this a complete secret until then."

He should have been ecstatic. And he was…sort of. What had he expected? A personal message? After the way he'd come on to her at the party?

He clicked on the attachment. He had to hand it to Gina and her camera crew; it made even *him* want to see the movie (and he was sick to death of the dialogue he'd memorized).

What to say in response? *How about an apology*, he thought. How about *I miss talking to you*?

He *did* miss her—and her girls. And they *had* promised to remain friends after the production wrapped. But he hadn't been acting like a friend…

Before he could second-guess himself, he dialed her number. "Gina, it's Zac."

"Zachariah! I'm so glad you called." She sounded breathless. "When I saw you at the party, I was a little inebriated, and I said some things…"

"I was going to say the same thing to you."

"I hope I didn't hurt your feelings," she said.

"We actors are used to being rejected," he said.

"Oh, Zac, I didn't mean—"

"I'm teasing," he said. "Actually, I called to apologize to *you*. I was out of line and I made you uncomfortable. Although…you *are* a very desirable woman, Gina."

There was a long moment of silence, and Zac thought he'd blown it again. But then that breathy voice came back. "Thank you."

"You're welcome," he said. "Now about the trailer…"

"Trailer?"

"The movie trailer you just sent…"

"Oh, *that* trailer!" she chuckled.

"It's very good," he said. "But I seem to recall a certain conversation about a beach scene…"

She laughed. "Zac, you can't be serious!"

"Don't you remember that discussion?" he teased.

"What I remember was…"

It felt good to have their friendship back on track. Even better because they could talk about their shared experience with *True Surrender*. And they did…

*   *   *   *   *   *   *   *   *   *   *   *   *

When the movie trailer for *True Surrender* went live five days later, Zac was thrust into a new phase of his life. He had press events and appearances with Lydia. Paparazzi started showing up wherever he went. He met with his agent to go over auditions and scripts. For the first time in his life, they were coming to *him*, just as Gina had predicted, and he couldn't stop marveling at it.

His agent said he should choose his next project before the premier of *True Surrender*. It had never been a problem finding projects he wanted to be involved with, but now he found himself unsure. He'd read a script and wonder: what would Gina think of it? Would she say it would push him to be bettter? Would she say it was a worthy endeavor? He found himself wishing he could ask her opinion, but he knew she was up to her neck in post-production on *True Surrender*.

At night, when he was tired of reading scripts but not tired enough to sleep, he would watch Gina's movies. He'd researched and found every film she had been involved with. Her first as director hadn't been a commercial success, but the second was the blockbuster that made Jed Landry into a celebrity. That actor had been one of Zac's models when he'd been studying. Interestingly, there was a long gap after that film before her name re-surfaced.

When the empty feeling or melancholy mood threatened to overcome him, instead of drowning it with alcohol or female company, he went for a walk. He rediscovered the parks nearest his apartment, and sometimes he'd lie in the grass and stare at the sky, imagining Gina doing the same on the deck of her house.

chapter 37

"Zac, this is Sylvester. I need you to come to my office right away."

Sylvester's office was on the other side of town.

"Why?" Zac said. "What's up?"

"We have a legal issue," Sylvester said. "And it concerns you. I'll see you here in an hour."

Zac hung up. The man was something else. What kind of legal business would require him to be ordered to Sylvester's office on the spur of the moment? Regardless, he got dressed and made the drive across town.

The receptionist sent Zac straight into a conference room. He was surprised to find Jeff, his lawyer, there as well as another tall man.

The tall man rose from a chair as Sylvester turned from the window and said, "Zac, this is Kurt Wrenshall from PR." The man held out his hand, and Zac shook it.

"Please, have a seat," Kurt said.

Zac did.

"I'm going to get straight to the point," Jeff said. "Sasha is claiming that you got her pregnant. Is this true?"

Zac gaped at the man. "She's saying *what*?"

"She claims she miscarried, and that the emotional toll is what led her to poison you."

Zac was unable to form a response.

"Is there a possibility she could have gotten pregnant by you?" Jeff said.

"No," Zac said.

"You were having sex?"

"Of course," Zac said. "We were a couple. But we weren't in *love*. We used protection."

"Is it possible you could have forgotten that protection in the heat of the moment?" Jeff said. "Even just once? Or that it may have broken? Or malfunctioned?"

"No!" Zac cried. "I would have known!" He meant he would have known if she'd been pregnant, but he doubted the other men would understand that.

"She says she miscarried alone, scared and traumatized," Jeff said. "There doesn't appear to be any physical evidence."

"Of course not!" Zac was stunned. "Because it never happened."

He turned to Jeff. "You're the lawyer. How can she make this sort of claim without proof?"

"The fact is, she can say whatever she wants to say," Kurt said.

"The claim is bogus!" Zac said. "It's fucked up! *She's* fucked up!"

"I happen to agree with you," Jeff said. "With the proof we now have that she poisoned you, she's headed for jail. I think this accusation is a last-ditch ploy, and from a legal standpoint, I don't think it can go anywhere."

"Then why I am here?"

"Because her accusation has larger ramifications," Sylvester said.

"You have to understand, from a PR standpoint, this could get ugly," Kurt said. "Her lawyers may try to establish that you have a pattern of short-term relationships, of one-night stands. They may even find women who will testify that you had sex with them. In short, this sort of accusation has the potential to destroy your reputation."

Abruptly Zac propelled himself out of the chair. "And my career."

"Casting directors may not want an actor associated with a negative reputation," Kurt said. "You may find you have fewer offers."

Zac stood at the window, rubbing his hand over the back of his neck. He had worked so hard...and for what? To have it destroyed by the same woman who'd tried to kill him? A hot heaviness spread through his chest.

"And because you're an integral part of this film that so many people have worked hard to create, whatever you say and do will have a direct impact on its success," Kurt said.

Zac heard Gina's words in his head: *I need* True Surrender *to be a success.* That more than anything gave him the control to take his seat again.

"The people in this room need to decide on a plan of action and each do their part in it," Kurt said.

Zac nodded his agreement. But when Sylvester said, "What about paying her to keep quiet?" he bolted from his chair as if touched by a live cattle prod.

"Absolutely not!"

"I'm just saying— "

"I will not," Zac said. "That's like admitting it happened. And it didn't!"

"You're emotional right now," Jeff said. "Take a day, calm down, think about your relationship, and we'll talk tomorrow."

"I don't need to think." Zac's voice had gone stone cold. "There is no *relationship*. She nearly *killed* me, and I've done my best to be fair to her anyway. If she wants to play hardball, then so be it. You hit her with every charge you can think of in relation to my poisoning." He yanked his sleeve up. "Because there's sure as hell *proof* of that!"

He stomped out of the room, slamming the door behind him.

He slammed his car door too. Then he slammed his fist against the steering wheel.

The lying bitch!

He threw the car into gear and squealed out of the parking lot. He turned the radio on full blast, then rummaged in the glove compartment. It had been a long time since he'd had a cigarette…

A car honked and he jerked the wheel to bring himself back into his lane. "Damn it!"

A liquor store appeared on the right and he swerved hard to enter the lot.

He found what he was looking for and got back in his car. He lit a cigarette and took a long drag. *Fuck it*, he thought. He popped the top off the bottle of Jim Beam and drank directly from it.

Without consciously deciding to do so, he started the car and pointed it toward the beach.

He parked at an overlook. Since it was 1:00 on a weekday, the place was empty. He took another long drag on the bottle, then on the cigarette. He gripped the steering wheel tightly, then dropped his head onto it.

She will destroy me one way or another.

He held his left arm out flat, his hand fisted, staring at the lumps that were the fistula. This was his reality now.

Thanks to HER.

The liquid hate sat heavy in his chest.

And she had threatened those he cared about. Threatened them still. She could destroy Gina's dreams as well…

His vision blurred. *Oh God Oh God Oh God.*

Unable to stay still, he got out of the car. Bottle and cigarette in hand, he headed toward the water. He started to run.

He ran faster, then faster still, as fast as he could go, until he tripped on a piece of driftwood and sprawled flat on his face in the sand.

"Fuck!" he screamed, and punched the sand. "Fuck! Fuck! Fuck!"

He picked up the driftwood and whipped it into the surf, swearing again. Then he fell to his knees, gasping for breath. He clutched at his chest, which was screaming fire.

He sprawled on his back, chest still heaving. A gull passed overhead, squawking at him. His hand touched the liquor bottle. He sat up, drawing his knees—and the bottle—to his chest.

The sun was setting when he stumbled back to the overlook. He fell against the side of the car, resting his head on the roof, cognizant enough to know he shouldn't drive but unable to care.

Through the window he glimpsed the green shirt that Gina had given him. He wrestled the back door open, then crawled inside and sprawled on the back seat. He grasped the green shirt tight to his chest.

chapter 38

"Hello Zachariah."

Even over the phone, the way Gina said his full name made the base of his spine tingle.

"There's something I need to talk to you about." Zac took a deep breath. "You're going to hear things about me, and I want you to know they're not true."

"Like the fact that you got Sasha pregnant?"

Wow, news really travels fast.

"Only, I didn't."

She was silent, and he rushed on. "I couldn't have. I decided early on that the only person I would go unprotected with would be The One. Sappy, yeah, but only true love could get me to give up the condoms."

He forced himself to stop. When he'd woken that morning in the back seat of his car with the green shirt draped over him, his first thought had been *what will Gina think?*

After a few moments, she said, "I believe you."

Relief washed over him.

"What are you going to do about it?" she said.

"When I first found out I was so angry." He paused; she might have suspicions but no way was he going to share more. "All I wanted to do was lash out. Now I don't know what to do. But it seems obvious I can't do *nothing*. Everything is going to go public, about the poisoning and all."

"I just wanted to let you know I'll do my best to keep your name out of it," he continued. "But someone might be able to track down where I spent those two weeks recuperating—and they might make insinuations."

"Probably." She sounded thoughtful. "How do you feel about the world knowing your personal business?"

He hadn't really had time to think about that aspect yet. "It's the price of fame, right?" he tried to joke.

"Too bad you couldn't enjoy the good stuff at least a little before you had to deal with a PR nightmare," she said. "You're going to need professional help."

"Sylvester wanted me to use his firm's guy," he said. "I turned him down. I figure his priority is going to be the production, not me."

"Smart move." There was another pause in the conversation. "But you're going to need PR help, and you're going to need it fast. As soon as the tabloids get wind of this, they'll be all over you."

He sighed.

"I might have a contact for you," she said. "She's good and she's got some ethics. I could see if she's interested."

"I would really appreciate that," he said. A referral from someone he respected as much as Gina was worth money to him.

"I'll give her a call as soon as we hang up," she said. "I'll email you her contact info if she's interested."

chapter 39

Gina had known it was coming. But it was still a mild shock to see Zac's face taking up the entire cover of *Fame and Fortune* magazine, with "Exclusive Interview Reveals All!" splashed in big red letters kitty-corner across the top.

She knew Zac had agonized over how much he wanted the world to know about his personal business. The only reason he'd agreed to this was because of the ridiculous coverage of Sasha's false claim.

Cindy had practically written the article herself as part of the exclusivity deal—and keeping Sylvester and company happy. Even Gina had a hand in it after Sylvester charged her with picking some set photos.

This could be a game-changer, that was for sure. She settled into her favorite easy chair, imagining women all over doing the same.

The first thing she noticed was the photos. Well, one photo in particular. In it, Zac sat on a rock, head propped in hand, staring intently at the camera...and he was wearing a familiar green shirt.

That can't be; surely the photographers would have insisted on controlling his wardrobe.

But no...it was *that* shirt, all right. And damn if it didn't turn her on despite all admonition to herself. Those penetrating blue-green eyes just about jumped off the page. She tore her eyes from that photo to check out the others. The photographers (not to mention the makeup folks) had done a bang-up job. They'd even gotten one of him with his shirt unbuttoned, showing the defined pecs she still remembered against her cheek that night.

But never his left arm, she noticed.

She moved on to the article itself.

The ring of her cell phone startled her, but she had to smile when she checked the caller ID. It was almost as if he had ESP.

"Zachariah."

"Holy shit, I'm looking at it right now," he said.

"The article?"

"What have I done?" He sounded freaked out.

"It's very well done."

"So you read it?" he said.

"I just finished."

"Oh man..." he breathed.

"This was all coming out anyway, right?"

"Right." But he didn't sound convinced.

"This way *you* controlled the spin," she said. "And the parts about Sasha are handled well. Heck, it even makes you out as the calm, cool and collected one with nary a pissed-off thought in your head."

He was silent but she could hear him breathing. "Zac?"

"Yeah," he said. "It's just a whole lot to...to share with people who don't even know me, who can't possibly understand..."

"I know."

"Do you know I had some crazy fan outside my door this morning?" he said.

She knew he was touchy about that after the Sasha thing, so she went for a lighter angle. "Well, was she cute?"

"It was a *he*!"

Gina couldn't help it; she laughed out loud.

chapter 40

"You see this, Gina?" Sabrina tossed a copy of one of the popular gossip magazines on the counter as she came around the bar.

Gina picked up the magazine. At the lower left corner a picture of Zac was overlaid with a teaser headline that read ZAC'S NEW LOVE! Her stomach clenched even as she reminded herself this was the paparazzi at work. Their job description was to make something out of nothing.

"Page 36." Sabrina joined Gina, Willow and Andie at their usual table at The Iron Zebra.

"Ever helpful," Gina muttered. Nevertheless, she flipped to page 36.

Her heart sank. There were several pictures. One was Zac exiting a trendy Hollywood nightclub with a gorgeous blonde. The blonde's arm was looped through Zac's and they leaned toward each other as if sharing a secret laugh.

The other picture was even harder to look at. Zac leaned against a door frame, looking relaxed and slightly disheveled. The blonde was leaned into him, her hand on his waist, her head tilted up, obviously in the process of kissing him.

"I can't believe you didn't tell us he was your famous actor," Willow grumbled. "All that time we thought he was just some random relative."

"I said I was sorry," Gina said.

"What good is having a famous director as a friend if you never get to meet anybody famous?" Willow said.

"Get over it," Sabrina said. "I want to see what she thinks about the article."

All three women were watching Gina. She scanned the article. *Zac and Katie have been friends for some time… both actors have recently starred in…*

She dropped it back on the counter.

"So, what do you know?" Sabrina said.

"Absolutely nothing," Gina said disgustedly. Had he heard one word she'd said to him about being true to himself?

"Could all be made up," Andie said.

"Pictures don't lie," Gina said. "He's a boy. He's still thinking with the other head."

He had a right to date anyone he wanted. And why shouldn't he? Just because he'd said those things about being attracted to her? It wasn't like he was going to pine away for someone who'd turned him down…

"We saw you guys at the patriot event," Sabrina said.

Gina flushed. "I had too much to drink that night."

"So you let your inhibitions down," Willow said. "And your true desire showed through. That boy felt the same."

"He was acting, Willow," Gina said. "That's what he does, remember?"

"Why would he *act* attracted to you when he could have any woman he wants?" Andie said.

"He did it for me," Gina said. "Which was nice, and I enjoyed myself. But you know how I feel about actors."

"Yeah," Willow rolled her eyes. "Those evil actors. Strictly off-limits from a romance perspective. So maybe you should just screw him."

"What!" Gina said. "Like some star-struck, bobble-headed fan?"

Willow smirked. "That is your true desire, isn't it? Why not get it out of your system? How long has it been, anyway?"

Gina frowned at her.

"Hmm," Sabrina picked up the magazine. "He didn't strike me as the blond bimbo type."

"Fame changes people."

I ought to know.

She'd spent her share of time with Beautiful People. Many of them men who expressed their desire for her. Most of them not the least bit beautiful where it really mattered. As a result she was rarely tempted to encourage their attention.

Until Jed. When they'd met, he had that something special that made him truly beautiful both inside and out.

Then came *Fame.* Watching that beautiful thing twist and change, and die a slow death nearly killed her, too. She'd held onto it, she'd fought it, she'd tried everything to save it...until that awful day she found him with Paula. She had mourned the loss of the inner beauty she'd fallen in love with as much as the institution of marriage.

After the time Zac had spent with her and the things he'd shared, she had dared to hope it might be different, that perhaps he would be strong enough to hold onto himself.

Apparently she was wrong. "Are we going to ride or yap?" she said.

Sabrina picked up her helmet. "Ride, Girlfriend!"

*   *   *   *   *   *   *   *   *   *   *   *   *

Gina's thoughts were still jumbled two days later when her phone indicated a call from Zac. She hadn't quite decided if she was going to give him a piece of her mind, but she answered anyway.

"Hello, Zachariah."

"I need you, Gina."

Gina's stomach dropped. The voice was Zac's but it didn't sound like him at all.

"Zac?"

"Something's gone wrong," he said. "The dialysis…a blood clot or an infection…doctor Carrini said it could happen…" Zac's words slurred, but she knew he hadn't been drinking. No, this was something more ominous than alcohol…

"Zac, where are you?"

"Home," he said.

Too far away!

"You need to call Mack," she said.

"I did."

"Is he coming?" she said.

"Don't hang up."

"I won't hang up, Zac," she said. "What did you tell Mack?"

"Every joint is on fire," he said. "Arms. Shoulders. Knees…"

"Zac, listen to me," she said. "What did Mack say? Did he say 'I'll be right there'?"

"He doesn't know."

"Doesn't know if he's coming?" she said.

"Doesn't know how bad it is."

Gina's stomach twisted. He must be running a high fever. He was lucid but not all altogether…*together*. But if *he* said it was bad…

"You're the only one who knows," he said. "Who really knows…"

But I'm too far away!

"Mack is coming, right?"

"Yes." The word was a sigh.

Relief lifted her momentarily.

"But don't hang up," he said. "I need you."

"I won't hang up, Zac," she said again.

He felt silent.

"Zachariah?" she said. "You still there?"

"It was made up, you know," he said.

"What was?"

"My *romance* with Katie," he said. "They made an assumption, and Cindy said…"

"What did Cindy say?"

"Just like with Sasha," he said. "All lies…none of it real."

He had a valid point, but she couldn't tell him that *now*. "Zac…"

"Acting is not just my job anymore," he said. "My life has become one big act…"

"You just don't feel good now—"

"I thought it would be so great…"

"It *is* great," she said. "You're very good—"

"No," he said. "Not when it means I can't have the one woman I truly want."

Gina didn't know what to say to that.

"You, Gina," he said. "I want something *real*. With you."

There was commotion on the other end of the line.

"Zac?"

"Mack…Mack is here," he said.

"Put him on the phone."

Shuffling sounds and muffled voices.

"Gina, as in Director Gina?" she heard Mack ask. Then: "Hello?"

"What's going on, Mack?" she said. "How does he look?"

"He's...ah shit."

"What?" she said. "What is it?"

"He's burning up."

"It must be an infection," she said. "The fever is the body's way of fighting it. You need to take him to Mercy Hospital in Encenito. Do you know how to get there?"

"Sure," Mack said.

"His doctor's name is Thomas Carrini," she said. "I'll track down his number and see if I can rustle up a welcoming party for you. And Mack?"

"Yes?"

"Please call me back when you get him there."

"Will do."

Gina found the information and made the call. After hanging up, she stood with the phone pressed to her chest for a long time. Then she sat down at her desk and stared at the computer screen without seeing it. She checked the clock. Went into the kitchen and poured herself a glass of juice. Stuck her phone in her pocket and stepped onto the deck.

How far was Zac's place from Mercy? She paced to the end of the deck and back. It was only 10 a.m. She paced again. She could be there in two hours if L.A. traffic wasn't bad. A third lap of the deck. Sabrina could watch the girls.

I need you, Gina.

She tossed her glass in the sink and grabbed her car keys. She would call Sabrina from the car.

*   *   *   *   *   *   *   *   *   *   *   *

She made the drive in under two hours. She took the elevator to the seventh floor and found Mack in the family lounge just as he'd said he would be.

"You must be Gina."

"And you must be Mack."

He held out his hand and she took it. "Wish we could have met under better circumstances," he said.

She nodded. "But it sounds like Zac will be okay."

"Antibiotics," he said. "The wonder drug. Apparently your suspicion was correct about the infection."

Gina's eyes went to the door.

"He's in room 715," Mack said.

"I'll just check in on him." She edged toward the door. "Maybe we could grab a coffee after?"

"Sure."

Gina tried to ignore the wave of déjà vu that swept through her when she peeked into Zac's room. It was just like the night she'd brought him to the hospital: his left arm encased in the dialysis paraphernalia, IVs running to his right, machines beeping and whirring.

She moved into the room, surveying the machines until she found what she was looking for: *temp 100.8*. She wondered how high it had been when he'd called her.

She lowered herself onto the bed, transfixed by his strong neckline and angled jaw with its five o'clock shadow. His hair was long and dark and tousled, and a sheen of perspiration adorned his forehead.

She reached out to brush the wetness away.

He pulled in a breath, and his eyes opened slowly.

She watched as those blue-green eyes found hers. Watched as surprise flowed into them.

"You're here," he rasped.

She looked down at herself in mock surprise. "I guess I am."

A smile ghosted his face. His hand found hers. Slowly he raised their hands to his mouth and kissed the back of her hand.

"Excuse me," a voice said from behind her. "I'm here to relieve Mister Davies of this pesky dialysis machine."

Gina's eyes never left Zac's. "Mack and I are going to grab coffee," she said. "I'll come back in a little while."

He nodded, already losing the battle against the drugs and sleep.

chapter 41

Zac came awake with a start.

Gina!

Had he only dreamed that she'd come to him?

He checked his arm: no tubes. He found the call button.

The nurse was more interested in checking his vitals, but she promised to check the lounge for Gina.

Five minutes later he was contemplating going Against Medical Advice when Gina poked her head into his room. "You up for company?"

"From you, absolutely." He patted the bed beside him. "Just don't tell anyone else I'm here."

"You don't look too bad," she said as she took a seat next to him.

"I feel better than I expected," he said. "Just a lingering headache over my eyes."

What exactly did I say to her?

"So," he said. "What a mess this PR plan has become."

"What do you mean?"

"Well, for starters, the whole bloody world thinks I got one woman pregnant—"

"They don't think that, Zac."

"And now they think I've moved on to the next one," he continued. "That was a setup, you know. Katie."

"A setup by who?" she said.

"Katie and I have been friends since our early acting days," he said. "When she said she wanted to get together, I didn't think she meant as a *couple*. I wasn't even looking for a date."

"Well…" Gina was silent for a moment. "At least the pictures came out well."

He snorted. "She let slip to the paparazzi exactly where we'd be and when. Then she came on to me. Her timing is impeccable," he said bitterly. "They didn't use the shots of me pushing her away."

He paused. "She seemed to think 'having our names linked' would be good for both our careers. I thought she liked me for me. Is this what fame is like? Never knowing if someone is with you for *you*, or for what you can do for them?"

"Unfortunately there is some of that," Gina said. "Although you do get better at sniffing out the bullshit."

He stared at her for a moment, then took a breath and dove in.

"Look, I don't know exactly what I said to you, but I have a pretty good idea, and I meant it." He reached for her hand. "I'd like more than friendship with you."

She was silent for too long, but he forced himself to hold his own silence.

Finally she spoke, her voice hushed. "I'm attracted to you, too. And I know if we got together it would be good. But…" She took a deep breath. "I don't do casual very well, I'm afraid. The physical piece is just not enough for me."

"You don't think much of me, do you?" he said.

Surprise clouded her eyes. "Why would you say that?"

"You think that's all I want from you?" he said.

"I think you're young, Zac," she said. "I think you have plenty of living to do, and time to decide what you really want. Heck, you might decide you want your own kids, which is something I'm unable to do even if I wanted to."

"So it's the age thing?" he said. "Seriously? I'm not some wet-behind-the-ears eighteen-year-old."

"You know and I know that you get one chance to make it big in this business. And you're *there*, Zac. You worked hard for it. You went through some serious shit for it." Her eyes darted to his arm. "You deserve it. And I think you need time to experience it. But...fame will change you. There's no way around that."

"The last time I got involved with an actor it didn't end well," she said. "I didn't just lose my heart. I lost a life partner and the father of my children. And I walked away from a promising career. At this point in my life I just can't do that again. The pictures and the rumors alone..."

She stopped; he tried but failed to read the thoughts behind her eyes. "What I want from a man is not fair to ask of you," she finally said.

"What you're really saying is that you don't think I can give it," he said.

Gina looked down. "Maybe it's not fair to ask it of anyone..."

"Gina, I—"

She silenced him with two fingers soft against his mouth. "Please don't." She looked sad. "There's something beautiful in you, Zac. My ex-husband had it, too. But fame killed it. Watching that die a slow death was almost worse than finding him in bed with another woman. I just can't do that again. And I won't ask you to walk away from your chance. I hope you understand."

He was at a loss for words.

"I've got to get back to the girls," she said. "Will you text or email me when you get home so I know you're okay?"

He nodded.

Then she did something completely unexpected. Her fingers drifted to his jaw and she leaned in to kiss him.

This kiss was entirely different than the others they'd shared. It was a simple press of her lips against his, soft but somehow so powerful it made something hurt deep in his chest. She lingered, just a little bit, and he opened his eyes in time to catch her rapid blinking, eyes glistening.

"I'll see you at the premier," she said.

All he could manage was, "Yes."

She squeezed his hand once and was gone.

chapter 42

"Thanks Mack." Zac dropped his gym bag on the couch.

"That's what friends are for," Mack said. "So what's going on between you and that director of yours?"

Zac sighed. "I wish I knew."

"So something did happen," Mack said. "And you didn't tell me!"

"There was nothing to tell," Zac said.

Mack paced the room. "That explains a lot."

"What does?"

"Ever since you got back from that shoot you've been different."

"Mack, I was poisoned, I was doing dialysis," Zac said. "I've been dealing with Sasha's accusations and this PR explosion..."

"Yeah," Mack said. "But that's not all. You go to the park instead of the bar. You hardly drink at all. And come to think of it, you haven't even *looked* at a woman—"

"Maybe I've just outgrown that stuff."

"Why did you call Gina?" Mack stopped directly in front of Zac and pinned him with a stare. "Yesterday, when you knew I was already on my way?"

"I don't know," Zac said. "I had a fever of a hundred and five. I wasn't thinking clearly. I don't even remember everything I said."

Mack gave him a *come-off-it* look. "Are you in love with her?"

"No. Yes." Zac ran a hand through his hair. "I don't know. What is love, anyway?"

"You have a better idea than many," Mack said.

"What do you mean?"

"Your parents," Mack said. "They were devoted to each other. Talk about a shining example. Do you have any idea how lucky you were?"

"I was *lucky* to lose my parents at fifteen?" Zac's voice rose.

Mack met Zac's gaze with a defiant one of his own. "You were lucky to have them for the time you did. Maybe if you focused on that instead of their death you wouldn't sabotage your own chance for love."

When he put it that way... Zac heard Gina's words too: *Now it's about you.*

"Why do you think I was always over at your house?" Mack continued. "Your parents were as different from mine as it was possible to be. It's because of your parents that I even *believe* in love. I was devastated when your parents died. Not like you, of course, but...I needed that example in my life. It was almost as bad as losing my best friend...which I did, you know, for that time."

Zac stared. "Mack, I didn't know..."

"I'd give my right arm to have something like that," Mack said. "Why do you think I've been holding out all these years?"

"I guess I thought..."

"You thought I was like you?" Mack said.

"Well...yeah."

They fell silent.

"So, back to Gina," Mack said.

"She's got every reason in the book why we shouldn't be together," Zac said.

"So you convince her otherwise," Mack said. "That is, if you believe she's worth it."

"Oh, she's worth it and more."

"Well, then, what's the plan?" Mack said.

Zac thought for a moment. "The premier. It's my best chance. And Igor."

Mack looked at him quizzically. "Who is Igor?"

"An agent," Zac said. "I gave him Gina's script."

"Gina's script?"

"Yeah." Zac reached for the phone. "You wouldn't believe it, but Gina can actually write, too. He should have read it by now. I hope he's got good news for me..."

chapter 43

Zac knew there'd be paparazzi surrounding all the premier events, but he hadn't counted on it keeping him so busy on this day, the day *before* the premier. Man, he'd barely said hello to Gina before his agent was whisking him into photo sessions and interviews.

It was all so distracting and a worthless use of time.

It was after nine o'clock when he was finally able to corner Gina in a small conference room away from the crowds.

"Gina, there's something I've got to tell you," he said. "Some exciting news."

"More exciting than the movie premier tomorrow?" she laughed.

"Yes," he said. "I showed your manuscript to Igor Skymane. He's an old friend from my college days. He read it, and he wants to talk to you about it. He might even want to represent you, to pitch the manuscript to—"

"Wait!" She shook her head as if she couldn't comprehend what he'd just told her. "You're telling me you took *my* manuscript, from *my* house, without my permission?"

"You've got to share this with the world."

"The world?" she said. "The world has plenty in it without me."

"That's why you live way out there, isn't it?" he said. "You're afraid of the world, afraid of rejection. You can't hide forever, Gina."

"You don't know jack about why I'm where I am," she said. "You think it was easy coming back to this job, this industry, after it took everything from me?"

"Hollywood didn't do that," Zac said. "Your ex-husband did. *One* person, Gina."

"Damn it, Zac, it was a fight I didn't want to have, but you know what? I'm damn good at it."

"That you are," he said.

"Did it ever occur to you that I had plans for that script?" she demanded. "And that those plans just might include my own production company?"

He reeled back.

"No," she said. "Because you didn't think it was important to ask me."

"It's brilliant," he said slowly.

"No, it's not," she snapped. "It's a pipe dream. But it's *my* dream. And you had no right to barge in on it."

"It never occurred to me…"

"Zac! There you are!"

Reluctantly, Zac turned toward the interruption.

"We're late," his agent said. "We've got to go. You're expected for an autograph signing in twenty minutes."

Zac turned back to Gina, but she was already moving away. He sighed; *that* sure hadn't gone the way he'd pictured it.

* * * * * * * * * * * * *

Gina returned to her hotel room after a low-key dinner with the crew, a distraction she'd been thankful for. Seeing Zac in his world, with the cameras and the journalists and the fans, had been jarring enough. Then his news about her manuscript... She wanted to stay mad at him, but really... He believed in her manuscript that much?

She nearly stepped on a folded piece of paper just inside her door. She picked it up.

Gina,

I'm sorry. I thought I was doing you a favor. I see now that I was wrong. But I stand by what I've said: your script is brilliant. And if anyone could pull off self production, it would be you. Would you let me buy you breakfast tomorrow to make up for it? There's a little café around the corner that should hide us from the hordes. I'll be there at 7:30. Hope to see you.

Zachariah

chapter 44

There was no excuse for the fact that she was five minutes late. She'd spent the night tossing and turning, feverish with desire, dreaming of Zac—wild, sexual dreams that mixed with images of him from the hospital, from the biker party, and from the film.

When she entered the café, he was staring out the window and didn't see her right away. He was wearing that green shirt again, and when he turned toward her, those blue-green eyes jumped right out at her. *Her*. He smiled, and her heart stopped.

God, he was sexy. On screen and off, although it was a different kind of sexy. Images from her dreams rose up and she felt herself flush with heat. Yes, she was in serious lust with this man.

Yeah, you and forty thousand fans.

Her feet took her toward him without conscious thought. He stood and held out his hands. "Does this mean I'm forgiven?"

She let him take her hands; it was like warm liquid flowing up her arms...and down to other places. She nodded, not trusting her voice.

He gestured to the table, and she sat. He slid into the seat across from her.

"I'm sorry I came down on you," she said. "It was really sweet of you, in a way. To believe in my story, I mean. I guess I need to believe in it more myself."

He nodded but didn't say anything. *Probably afraid to*, she thought.

After a moment, he said, "What are the girls up to these days?"

She told him about Christine's new boyfriend (not the boy she went to the dance with) and Allie's horseback lessons. It felt good to be the reason for the smile on his face.

Then he sobered. "Gina..." He looked down at his hands on the table, then reached across the table as if to take hold of her hands.

"Excuse me." A woman's voice spoke above her head. Gina looked up to find a 30-something woman standing over their table, staring at Zac. Gina hadn't even seen her coming.

"You *are* Zac Davies, aren't you?" The woman said.

Gina noticed a flicker of annoyance cross Zac's face before it settled into his actor's mask. He turned to the woman.

"You are!" The woman's voice rose. "Oh, my God, you're Zac Davies! I am *such* a fan! I've got to get your autograph. No, a picture! Could I get a picture with you?" The woman started digging for her smart phone.

"Zac Davies is here?" Another voice said. And before Gina knew it, there were several women surrounding Zac, hemming him in, sucking all the air out of the space around him.

He kept his game face on. "Ladies, I'm trying to have a quiet breakfast here."

The response was more squealing from near the café entrance, then the sound of pounding feet. The first woman reached out, as if to grab his arm, and Zac came up out of his seat.

Gina stood, too. As if in slow motion, she saw the woman reach for Zac's left arm...Zac fend her off with his right, holding his left protectively away from the woman.

Gina knew how sensitive he was about that arm. All her protective instincts went into overdrive. "Hey!" she shouted. "Keep your hands off him!" But what could she do, short of yanking on the woman's hair? This was the price of fame, after all.

"Ladies, ladies!" The café manager pushed his way into the small throng of women. "Don't make me call the cops! Be orderly and ask nicely or you're out of here!" He turned to Zac. "I do apologize, Mister Davies."

"Not your fault," Zac said tersely.

"Maybe we should leave," Gina said.

"No," Zac said. "I would like to finish my breakfast."

"Okay." Gina shrugged and sat.

"No photos," Zac said. She watched as he made quick work of signing autographs, the café owner hovering over the women.

"You got what you wanted from Mister Davies," the owner said. "Now leave him in peace!"

Grumbling, the women headed for the door, and Zac finally took his seat.

"Fame," Gina said shakily. It had been awhile since she'd been close-up on a fanatic fan.

"I'm sorry," he said.

"Not your fault," she said.

It took him a moment to catch on, and then he gave her a relieved smile. He sighed and looked at his watch. "I have to go," he said regretfully. "I've got that radio interview this morning. Sylvester will kill me if I'm late."

He stood, obviously reluctant, and placed several bills on the table.

"I think I'll stay and finish my coffee," she said. "Now that your fans are gone, it's a nice quiet place."

"I'll see you at the press event then." Zac hesitated, as if he wanted to say something more.

"Yes, press event," she said.

He nodded, then turned and walked out. She couldn't tear her eyes from his ass. And the dreams were back again, too; she felt herself growing wet at the thought of Zac's hands on her...

She had not wanted a man this way in...well, possibly ever. Part of it was that she hadn't had sex in a long time...but it was more than that. It was *him*. Would it be using him? He'd made no secret of the fact that he desired her. No, she concluded. Just two consenting adults getting what they wanted.

What she needed. What she deserved. Why was she denying herself, anyway? She could have him now, while he was still beautiful...

A one-night stand. That's all it had to be. It's not like she hadn't done that before. Well, only once or twice... when she was younger. And no one would ever have to know...

She stared out the window, thinking she should head back to the privacy of her hotel room.

And then she saw Sasha.

chapter 45

Gina did a double-take. Had she really seen what she thought she'd seen?

It can't be.

Both she and Zac had restraining orders for Sasha. And she couldn't be crazy enough to be here now, during the premier... could she?

Gina stood abruptly and gathered her purse. She let herself out onto the sidewalk and stood there, the sense of unease still strong. She looked both directions, then studied the shops across the street. It was still early and there were few people about.

Ridiculous, she thought. *My imagination getting the better of me... in more ways than one!*

A couple hours later she met Sylvester and his entourage in the hotel conference room. Things got hectic when the catered lunch arrived only moments before Zac and Lydia (and their entourage). Servers were coming and going, people were eating on the run, and everyone was talking a mile a minute.

Zac and Lydia were, of course, the center of it all; even if she'd wanted to tell Zac about her odd moment in the café, there was no time.

"Listen up!" One of the PR folks called out. "I need director, writer and lead actors in the prep room *now*!"

The prep room was blessedly quiet. The PR person handed them each a cue card. "Zac, you're going to introduce the director, and Lydia the writer. Take a few minutes to get those lines down. I'll be back in a minute to hear 'em." The door closed behind her.

"Let's see what great things I get to say about you," Zac teased Gina.

Gina heard the door click open, then closed. She didn't think anything of it until it was followed by the sound of a bolt sliding into place.

Gina turned to find the barrel of a gun aimed directly at her chest. She must have made a sound (though her brain froze instantly), because Zac and the others turned too.

"Sasha!" Zac said.

"I might have known you'd be with *her*." The gun's aim didn't change, even though Sasha's eyes shifted to Zac. "You've been carrying on with her all this time. Two-timing me since the filming started!"

Zac's look turned to one of confusion. "What are you talking about? It was over between us before filming even started."

"I saw you!' Sasha said. "The two of you, in that café, holding hands!"

The gun dipped as Sasha focused her attention on Zac. "We were so good together, you and me. You told me so."

As she spoke Zac subtly shifted his body to try and shield Gina's.

"I only wanted you to love me back," Sasha continued. "I never meant to hurt you. I wouldn't do that. It was an accident. We were so happy together. We can still be happy…"

Gina finally found her voice. "Sasha, you need help."

"Don't talk to me *bitch*!" The gun—and Sasha's focus—was

back on Gina. "This is all your fault. Taking him away like you did. You're going to pay for this. Once you're out of the way, Zac will love me again, and *only* me."

"Sasha!" Zac's voice was sharp. "You want to talk about love? Then let's talk about love."

Gina felt his hand against her hip, trying to push her behind him. "What you did to me was not love, Sasha. Love would never feed me *poison*. You want to see what your kind of *love* looks like?"

Even in her dazed state, Gina recognized the undercurrent of rage in Zac's voice, and her panic grew.

Zac stepped toward Sasha, unbuttoning his sleeve as he did so. "You want to see what you did to me?"

Zac pushed this arm toward Sasha, and she took a step backward. Gina recognized the first inklings of fear on Sasha's face and knew that at some level she must have also recognized Zac's anger.

"You see that?" Zac said. "You see what your love is? You want to know what it feels like to have needles shoved into your arm three times a week? You want to know what color blood is when it's taken out of your body?"

He took another step toward Sasha, and Gina wanted to grab at his arm, hold him back...but she was powerless to move.

"*Look at it!*" He commanded.

Sasha shook her head; the gun trembled in her hand.

"I'll tell you what," he continued in a quieter voice. "I'm going to give you a close-up look..."

He started to tear off the bandage that covered his fistula. Sasha's eyes darted to his arm.

Lightning quick, Zac swung his hand hard. The gun clattered to the floor, and Lydia screamed.

At the same moment there was a loud *BANG* on the door.

"Open up!"

But Zac had grabbed Sasha and his hands closed around her neck. His voice dropped to a growl. "I don't love you. I will *never* love you."

More banging and thumping on the door. Gina willed her body to move, but it still wouldn't respond properly. "Zac!" she said.

"And if you ever hurt the ones I *do* love..." he continued to growl as he forced Sasha to step back. Her hands grabbed at his and her eyes were wide with fear. "I will kill you."

Gina's feet finally obeyed her command to move, and she made a grab for Zac's arm. "Zac, stop!"

"*I will kill you,*" he repeated.

"Zac, please," Gina pulled on his arm. "Let go."

BLAM! The door to the room exploded from the outside in.

At the same moment, Zac released Sasha. She fell to the floor, gasping and holding her hands to her neck as police officers rushed in.

Zac turned, and Gina fell into his arms, her knees threatening to give out. He crushed her to his body. "Oh, God, Gina..." he breathed.

She was suddenly sobbing and gasping for breath.

"I'm so sorry, Gina, so sorry I got you into this."

She shook her head, unable to speak. *Christine...Allie... motherless...* She started to shake uncontrollably. Zac lowered her gently, holding her close, stroking her hair.

"Are you all right?" Someone put a hand on Zac's shoulder.

"I'm fine," he said, but she could feel a tremor in his body.

"Is she all right?" Gina heard Sylvester's voice.

"Does she look all right?" Zac's voice was sharp.

"Gina, honey, it's okay," Zac spoke gently in her ear. "It's over.

We're all okay."

She couldn't stop crying; it was as if all the pent-up emotions of the past months had swamped her. She was aware of people moving around them, of Sasha whimpering as she was handcuffed and lead away, but all she could do was cling to Zac, her tears creating an ever-wider puddle on his shirt.

Then Lydia was there, too, embracing her and Zac, her tears mixing with Gina's. And then Dave…all four of them on the floor in a huddle. It was their presence that gave Gina the courage to pull herself together. She lifted her face to Lydia and released her grip on Zac's shirt to hug her hard.

"How did you know?" She heard Sylvester ask.

"We had an anonymous call," Detective Gray said. "Someone on your cast or crew. Said they saw Sasha hanging around here."

Gina looked at Zac and knew he was thinking the same thing.

Candy.

chapter 46

Getting dressed and ready for the press event seemed like a monumental task, but Gina managed to do it. The crew and the PR folks seemed to understand her need for space, and she was grateful for the semi-private area they'd curtained off for her in the dressing room. She was also thankful for Suzie, because without Suzie her face truly would have scared the cameras.

Now she had a few moments alone, which was almost harder. *Don't think too much...*

The sound of a throat being cleared pulled her attention to the mirror. She found myself looking at Zac in his Class A uniform. Was that really the same costume he'd worn in so many of the scenes they'd shot? Because it looked a hell of a lot more sexy right now...

"I just wanted to make sure you're okay," he said.

She turned to him and held out her hands. "I think I've finally stopped shaking," she tried to joke.

He took both her hands in his. His hands were warm and strong, and she had a nearly overpowering urge to fold herself into him again.

"Nope," he looked up at her. "Still shaking."

"That's nerves now," she said, although she wasn't sure that's all it was.

His gaze dropped to their hands and his grip tightened.

She watched, at a loss for words, as he breathed in slowly, his chest expanding against the medals on his uniform. As if from far away, she heard the calls for Zac and Lydia to take their places.

Zac didn't move away; instead he met her gaze as he exhaled slowly. In his eyes she read the desire and the longing, and she wondered if he saw the same in hers.

"I *need* to see you," he said. "Tonight. After the premier. I don't care how late."

"Zac!" The voice called again. "Where the hell is Zac?"

"Damn it." He released one hand and raked it through his hair.

She had no will left to resist what her body so desired. "Yes," she said.

His gaze snapped back to hers.

"I'll come to you," she said. "Whenever you can get away."

"Midnight," he said. "My room. I'll be there."

To her surprise, he leaned toward her and brushed a light kiss on her lips. "I'll be waiting for you."

She felt his fingers slip from hers.

*   *   *   *   *   *   *   *   *   *   *   *   *

This is utter craziness, Zac thought as he stepped out of the limo. All he really wanted to do was get Gina alone…

He was blinded by camera flashes as he turned to help Lydia out of the car. Her nails dug into his arm as they posed for photos. It had been a long day for her too. The noise was deafening and he was sweating under his tuxedo. He focused on the long red carpet at his feet, following it into the building, smiling and waving blindly all the way.

He breathed a sigh of relief when they reached the inner sanctum. This was invitation-only territory, and seemed almost hushed after the chaos outside the doors.

And then Gina was there. "Zac! Lydia!"

She wore a full-length gown of shimmering gold that accented her dark hair and eyes. Her hair was swept up and curls cascaded around her face.

"Gina, you look…" Zac swallowed around the cottonball suddenly lodged in his throat. "Stunning."

"As do you, Zachariah." Her soft voice and the way his full name rolled off her tongue caused an unexpected shiver to move up his spine. Lydia still stood with her arm in his, but he hardly noticed.

"Gina, my girl!" A voice boomed.

One of the most strikingly handsome older men he'd ever seen pulled Gina into an embrace and gave her a big kiss on the cheek. Zac was instantly envious of the man's ease in touching her.

Isn't that…?

Gina caught him staring.

"Zachariah," she said, "I'd like to introduce you to my ex-husband, Jed Landry."

"Oh, I know who—"

Huh? Did she just say ex-husband?

Jed's hand was extended and Zac took it.

"Jed, this is Zachariah Davies."

"Nice to meet you," Zac said.

"The pleasure is mine," Jed said.

Gina's breakout film was Jed's breakout film…and they were married??

Jed held his hand a bit longer than necessary, as if he were sizing Zac up.

"So…you're here to support Gina?" Zac said.

Jed inclined his head. "That and the fact I backed the film."

Zac looked from him to Gina, then back again. "Why?"

"Because everything this girl touches turns to gold." Jed put his arm around Gina again. "Even people. You'll know what I mean very soon."

Zac looked at Gina and knew what she was thinking. Her definition of *gold* was very different from Jed's. Her voice held a hint of sarcasm. "It did take an entire cast and crew, Jed."

"Of course," Jed said. "But the right director can be the difference. I should know." He removed his arm from around Gina and pointed at Zac in a fashion Zac didn't much care for, as if issuing a silent challenge. "But it's what you do with it now that matters."

Zac held the man's gaze but said nothing lest his dislike show too clearly.

Jed waved to someone across the room. "Excuse me," he said.

Zac watched him go, waving his drink arrogantly, then turned back to Gina. "He's right."

"About what?" Gina said.

"I didn't *become* a star," he said. "You *made* me a star."

"Zac," she smiled. "No director can conjure up talent where there is none. I may have brought out something better in you, but I didn't make you a star. You found something within yourself that did that."

"And a whole lot of luck," Zac said.

She laughed. "Yes, some of that, too."

It's what you do with it now that matters.

* * * * * * * * * * * * *

Zac had lived as Aaron Bricewick for months. He had worked hard to capture each of those scenes. But seeing it come alive—in order, with the added drama of the lighting and the camera angles and the music—on that big screen, in that hallowed place, was humbling. Masterful.

Emotional.

When they got to the scene he'd practiced with Gina, he was suddenly swamped with the memory of her body pressed against his, her back against the wall…

Zac's eyes were drawn to Gina.

Lydia leaned into him. "I hope things work out between you and Gina."

He glanced at her, surprised. "How did you know?"

"I didn't know for sure," she smiled. "Until just now."

She patted him on the arm and turned back to the screen. Zac turned his attention back to Gina to find her eyes on him. She nodded, the smallest smile on her lips. He nodded back, a silent confirmation that he approved…confirmation of what they'd accomplished together.

Together…she wanted that, too. Why did she keep running from it?

chapter 47

Zac threw his jacket over the chair and loosened his tie, leaving it to hang around his neck. He poured himself another drink from his private stash and paced the room with the glass in his hand, not really interested in drinking it. He looked at his watch for the hundredth time, then took it off and tossed it on the dresser. Would she really come?

He started at the knock on the door. He swung it open—and was instantly swamped with desire.

Without a word, he stepped aside to let her in. As he closed the door behind him, she took several steps and turned to face him.

Zac knew what desire looked like…and it was there in Gina's face, her eyes, even her body. His mouth went dry. Without looking away from Gina, he reached one hand out to set the glass on the console.

Gina seemed to flow toward him. Her hand reached out and touched his shirt—and it was as if an electrical connection had been completed.

Her kisses were ravenous. Demanding. Dizzying. She ran her hands up over his shoulders and into his hair, pulling him even deeper into the kisses.

He ran his hands up her back, grasping at the buttons at the top of her dress.

She tugged his shirt out of his waistband and slid her hands up under them. He gasped at the sensation of her hands on his waist, his belly, his chest.

He ran his hands along her sides and under the swell of her breasts. She moaned softly when he brushed his thumbs across her swollen tips, and the sound brought another wave of desire… to taste her there…to taste her *everywhere*.

Her fingers worked the buttons of his shirt until she could push it back and off his arms. She moved her kisses to the sensitive crevasse of his collar bone.

He found the zipper of her dress, desperate to feel *more* of her against his belly. She broke contact only long enough to step clear of the fallen dress, and a small moan escaped him.

Then she was pressed against him again, the lace of her bra tickling his chest, the heat of her crotch teasingly close.

He was completely overwhelmed by her. The smell of her hair…the taste of her mouth as she nipped lightly at his lips… the feel of her hands slipping around to cup his ass. He groaned, knowing he'd already passed the point of no return. What had happened to the control he'd prided himself on?

Her hands were on his button, then his zipper…then inside his pants. "Please don't stop." His voice came out a desperate whisper.

"Zachariah." Her voice was husky against his ear, and a tremor moved through his body. But it was her next words that nearly caused his knees to buckle.

"I want you inside me."

Freed of his pants, he took her down on the bed.

*   *   *   *   *   *   *   *   *   *   *   *   *

Zac lay on his side with his arm stretched out beneath Gina's neck, her back tucked into his belly. She stroked his thumb, his hand, his wrist. When she reached the ridge of his arm graft, he instinctively tried to pull away.

"Don't." She tangled her hand in his so he couldn't move his arm. "This is a part of who you are."

She brought her lips to his arm, running her tongue lightly along the contours of the graft. That arm had been touched a thousand times over the last six months...and each of those touches had brought only pain. But *this*...with her every motion she was showing him what she felt.

He was wrecked, and he knew it. "It brought me to you." His voice was husky from emotion and exhaustion.

She tucked her head beneath his chin. Her hand stilled and her breathing evened out. He was on the brink of slumber himself when he whispered, "I love you, Gina Devereaux."

chapter 48

For the first time in a long time, Zac came awake with anticipation. But he quickly realized there was no warm body next to him. He sat up.

The shower. She's in the shower.

But there was no sound from the bathroom.

"Gina!" He yanked the sheet off himself and padded, naked, to the bathroom. The door was slightly ajar and it was clear she wasn't there.

A stirring of panic rose in his chest. As he turned back to the main room he saw it. A piece of paper—feminine scribbling on it—rested on the table.

"Oh no…"

He approached the note with trepidation. Hesitantly, he picked it up.

Zachariah,

I don't know what to say…"Thank you" seems inadequate for how you made me feel last night. But I

*can't let you waste your talent (and your chance)... and
I can't live in your world. I pray you'll understand.*

Gina

"No," he muttered, fisting the paper in his hand. "No, no, no, *no*!"

The paper fluttered to the floor and he fell onto the bed, dropping his head into his hands.

She had come to him so willing, so open, holding nothing back. Younger women held nothing next to her. Had he imagined her desire? Had he imagined all the things she said with her touch and her eyes?

No. And now that he had said those three little words to her, they were no longer so scary.

Why had he let her talk him out of it once already? He had listened to her reasons. He had gone back to his life and picked up where he left off. He had tried to convince himself his life was fine the way it was. That it was better than it had ever been; that (like she'd said) his dreams of fame and money were finally coming true.

But the moment he saw her at the hospital last week, he knew. He knew that his life wasn't complete. He knew that whatever 'fame' came his way, it wouldn't fill the empty place in his soul. Not the way Gina and her girls did.

"Oh, no, Gina Devereaux," he said to the empty room. "You don't get to decide this. Not this time. Not without including me."

chapter 49

Gina gripped the steering wheel until her knuckles were white.

After that first explosive release, she had explored Zac's body with abandon. She had watched him for a thousand hours or more on screen; she knew every plane of his body, every angle, every crevasse. But it was no substitute for the intoxication of him, the way he responded to her touch…

She had made good use of that knowledge, until he was moaning and begging for her. In the wee hours of the morning he had returned the favor, bringing her to climax over and over again: in the shower, on the bathroom counter, on the balcony…

She had done some difficult things in her life, but leaving Zac ranked right up there. The image of him as she'd left him was so vivid it hurt: the sheets twisted at his waist…the strong belly and chest…the dark hair at the nape of his neck. He was every woman's fantasy. It was that *body* she'd lusted after for months.

But it was the man inside that she'd fallen in love with.

How could she have fallen for another __actor__?

"Stupid," she muttered… and that started a fresh round of tears.

It was better to hurt now than when *IT* happened, she told

herself. Zac was going to have women throwing themselves at him. Younger, more beautiful women. Relationships would be forged on sets and tours. She'd been in film for twenty years; she no longer believed that a man could withstand that kind of constant temptation. What would she tell the girls when he left them for someone he loved more? They weren't three and five anymore; they weren't naïve like they had been when Jed left. They would be so crushed they might never recover.

And neither would she.

chapter 50

It was barely 9 a.m. when Zac knocked on Dale's hotel door.

Dale opened the door wearing only a bathrobe. "Zac?" His eyes were still bleary. "What the hell?"

"I need your help," Zac said. "May I come in?"

Dale looked at him for a long moment. "This have something to do with Gina?"

"As a matter of fact…yes."

Dale sighed, then held the door open. "Come on in, kid. Coffee's already started."

If Gina had said anything to anyone before leaving, it would be Dale.

Zac stopped just inside the door, embarrassed to see a man sprawled on the bed. Before he could say anything, Dale spoke. "You might as well meet my partner. Zac, this is James. James, Zac."

James held up a hand in a silent greeting.

"Shit, I'm sorry…" Zac said.

"James likes his sleep." Dale poured two cups of coffee and offered one to Zac. "We'll use the balcony."

They stepped out into an already-sultry but breezy day.

"So what's on your mind, kid?" Dale settled into a patio chair, and Zac followed suit. Now that he had disrupted Dale's morning, he felt off-point. It was obvious Dale wouldn't have talked to Gina before she left. But his need to get answers about Gina overrode his discomfort.

"I need to know about Jed Landry," he said. "What happened between him and Gina?"

"That's a pretty personal thing to ask," Dale said. "You need to know this because?"

"Because..." Was he actually blushing?

"So you spent the night with Gina." It was a statement rather than a question. "You had some mind-blowing sex...and now you think you're in love with her?"

"No...well, yes to the sex part, but..." He stared into the blue sky. "I fell in love with her months ago. When I saw who she really is. When I spent that time at her place, with her and her girls. No sex involved."

He looked directly at Dale. "When I told her how I felt at the end of filming, she turned me down. She pointed out our age difference, said we wanted different things out of life, said I needed to be free to grab my time in the sun. I let her talk me into that. I tried to go back to my life. But the minute I saw her again...I knew."

Dale was silent for a long time, just studying Zac. Finally he said, "I assume you know that Gina directed the movie that made Jed famous."

Zac nodded. "I realize that now. But until last night I didn't know *he* was her ex."

Dale looked surprised, but he continued. "They fought like cats and dogs through the shoot. Then fell madly in love. Well, Gina did, anyway. They got pregnant, so they got married. She put her career on hold to support his."

That explained the gap between films that he'd noticed earlier.

"But Jed is an actor. And actors..." He sighed. "No offense, kid, but this is how it is. You're passionate about *this* project... until it ends. Then you're passionate about *that* project...until it ends. You approach your personal relationships the same way. All passion...until it burns out."

Dale paused to look closely at Zac. "So the inevitable happened. Gina was at home with two babies, and Jed was having an affair. And not with just any woman; it was with Gina's best friend from college, who was also part of the cast. My guess is that he had other affairs, too, but if Gina knows, she's never said."

Some of this Zac already knew. "But she told me she'd forgiven Jed."

"Forgiving and *forgetting* are different things," Dale said. "I don't think a woman ever *forgets* that kind of betrayal. Especially not a woman as passionate as Gina."

Zac's mind flashed briefly on just one aspect of passion he'd witnessed in Gina that night.

"The thing is," Dale continued, "Everyone on that film knew about Jed's affair. Not a single person had the guts to tell Gina. And those were people that—up until then, anyway—she considered friends. Then when she confronted her so-called friends, they turned the table on her. Started false rumors about her."

"I never found any of that when I went over her background." Zac wouldn't go into detail on how he'd studied her work over the past months.

"They died out pretty quickly," Dale said. "Because everyone knew in their heart they weren't true. But she sure had to claw her way back into the industry. Not that I could ever figure out why she wanted to be there."

Zac had an idea why. "She loves it," he said. "And she's damn good."

"True," Dale said. "That's not why I'm loyal to her, though. I stick with her because of the person she is—all the time, whether on set or off. She doesn't let everyone see that, though. In Gina's mind there are no longer many *friends* on a film set."

Zac thought about how different Gina was at home than she was on set. "Guarded."

He didn't realize he'd said it out loud until Dale responded. "*Guarded* is a good description. She'll only let you in so far."

Dale's gaze bored into Zac's but he left the question unspoken. Instead he said, "What Gina wants and what she craves—and frankly, what she deserves—is a man—"

"With staying power," Zac finished.

Dale nodded. "So you've got to think about this carefully. If you can't be that kind of man, then you should leave her be."

"I don't need to think about it." Zac stared into the sky again, not really seeing anything. "I've been alone since I was fifteen. I don't mean I haven't been surrounded by people; there have always been friends and such... The projects take away the loneliness, but it always comes back. But those weeks at Gina's...I didn't feel that."

And suddenly he knew exactly why he hadn't chosen his next project yet.

chapter 51

Gina pressed the button on the TV remote, not really seeing anything on the screen. How would she occupy herself the rest of the day? What could she do to keep her mind off Zachariah Davies?

She heard Christine and Allie break into excited chatter. A moment later she heard muffled shouts and the pounding of feet on the steps outside. Wearily she pulled herself out of the recliner.

She looked out the kitchen window. Her heart raced. The car in her driveway… the voice outside…

It couldn't be!

Of their own accord, her feet carried her to the door. She stopped short when she saw her girls clinging to a very familiar figure. "Zac?"

"Gina." He straightened from the hug he'd been giving Christine and Allie.

She crossed the porch to the railing, stunned, trying to understand what she was seeing.

"Girls, I really need to talk to your mom alone," Zac said.

Christine and Allie looked at Gina, who was taking the steps in a fog.

"You won't leave, will you?" Allie said.

"I promise I won't leave without telling you," he said. "But how long I stay depends on your mom." His eyes sought Gina's, dark and penetrating.

Without a single comment, the girls took the stairs, looking back once before they disappeared into the house.

Gina was rooted to the spot as Zac came to within two feet of her. "You don't get to do this, Gina," he said. "You don't get to rock my world, tell me you love me and then walk away."

"I…" She stopped. "I did that?"

A smile tugged at the corner of his mouth. "Not in so many words."

He was so goddamn handsome she had to look away.

"Look, I know how you feel about actors," he said. "You think we all have short attention spans, that passion burns out fast. And it's true of many…including Jed."

He closed the gap between them and took her hand. The gesture sent tingles all the way up her arm.

"But I'm not Jed." His head bent to hers and his voice dropped low. "If you open your life and your heart to me, I promise I will never break it." Two strong fingers slipped under her chin and tilted it up. "You already have mine, you know. Please tell me I'll never be alone again."

She looked at him through tear-filled eyes. She had been wrong about him. Wrong to let him go. He was worth a risk, worth a fight…

Finally she managed to respond, her voice barely above a whisper. "Okay."

"Okay?" he said, as if surprised to encounter so little resistance.

She ran her hands up his arms and around his neck, trying to keep her emotions in check. "Just one question," she said. "Your career, your work…have you chosen your next project?"

"Actually, I have," he said, then hesitated.

She couldn't stand it. "Well, what is it?"

"What I'd really like to do is help you set up your production company and get your script into production."

Her mouth dropped open. "But...why?"

"I realized why I've been so driven to be an actor," he said. "It's because living someone else's life was preferable to living mine. I don't *need* to act. I don't feel that way anymore. And you know what? It feels pretty damn good."

Finally she found her voice. "But Zac," she said. "You're so good. Surely you can find roles you're interested in..."

"There's only one role I'm interested in."

"Oh?"

He pulled her close again. "The role of husband and stepdad. Here, with you."

She was so shocked her knees nearly gave out. This was nearly too much for her to absorb. "Are you *crazy*?"

"I knew you'd say that." He released her and reached into his pocket.

"What the—?" she started.

He held a small box in his palm. "I know you won't agree to marry me right now," he said. "You want to make sure I have staying power. But you need to know where I stand on this."

Almost gingerly, he opened the box. Inside was a simple etched gold ring. "It's a promise ring. My father gave it to my mother before they could afford anything else. It took me a long time to realize how deep their love for each other went. It's one of the few possessions I kept."

"Zac..." Tears welled in her eyes again.

"Whenever you're ready—whenever you say the word—I fully intend to replace it with a wedding band." He took the ring from its box and held it in his forefingers. "Just tell me you'll give me the chance to prove myself to you."

She was crying in earnest now. Her fingers shook as she touched the ring, then looked into those blue-green eyes. He slipped the ring onto her finger, his hands warm against hers. She pulled his mouth to hers for that sweet, sweet taste she craved. He folded her into him and gave her what she wanted, taking her breath away.

"Mom?"

Gina turned to find both her girls in the doorway.

"You're going to let him stay, aren't you?" Allie said.

"Oh yes," she smiled at Zac. "He can stay."

The girls whooped and cheered, nearly knocking Zac over with their hugs. When they finally turned to enter the house, he wrapped his arm around her and whispered, "Are you sure?"

She could see the very real longing in his eyes. She pressed her hand to his heart. "Welcome home, Zachariah."

epilogue:
18 MONTHS LATER

Zac followed Gina and the girls through the hotel's back hallways to the underground parking area. Their limousine waited there, untouched by the fanatical fans that lined the sidewalk between their hotel and The Marque. It was a little ridiculous to drive four blocks, but there was no way he'd trust Gina and the girls in that throng of people, bodyguards or not.

Every time he thought of the film—*their movie!* —he was astonished all over again. They had done it. Together.

Now if only she'd agree to set a date for the wedding...

He glanced at the other actors getting into their limos, then climbed in and settled himself next to Gina. Her hand found his. "Nervous?" he said.

"Very."

As tenacious as *Director* Gina was, it was endearing how vulnerable she was about her writing. This was her writing debut, after all. He squeezed her hand and leaned in for a kiss.

He looked at Christine and Allie. How grown-up they looked! Christine had a steady boyfriend, a terrific kid he and Gina both liked. But Allie...he was going to have to keep a close eye on *her* boys. "Crazy, huh?"

"This whole thing is...surreal," Christine said.

Gina's cell phone rang. "Yes? ... They're already there? ... Great." She hung up.

"Was that Candy?" Zac said.

Gina nodded. "Everything is going smoothly."

Asking Candy to become Gina's assistant had been a stroke of genius. Her loyalty to Zac was easily transferred to Gina and never in question. And the previously shy, mousy girl was blossoming in the role.

The limousine crawled its way toward The Marque. The girls craned their necks to watch as the actors stepped out of their limos.

And then it was their turn.

"Are you girls ready for this?" Zac said. "Remember, you're going to be blinded by the cameras. Just follow the red carpet."

They nodded. Zac stepped out first, and the crowd went wild. He smiled and waved into the flashes, then ducked into the limo and held his hand out. "You're on, girls!"

One at a time he helped them out of the limo. Christine and Allie froze momentarily. Then Gina's voice lifted over the crowd. "You go, girls!"

Zac saw Christine and Allie glance over their shoulders as he helped Gina from the limo. Gina was grinning from ear to ear, and the crowd was cheering. He thought his heart might bust right out of his chest.

Paparazzi called from behind the cords as they started their walk down that red carpet. "Zac! Over here! Gina! Give us a smile!"

"Zac, how do you feel about Miss Stone's newest request?"

Zac didn't answer the reporter; it seemed that the legal issues with Sasha would never end, but this was no time to dwell on that.

"So, when is the other big date?" Another reporter asked.

"That's a closely guarded secret," Zac said.

"Aw, come on. Your fans want to see the fairy-tale wedding."

"His fans are going to have to get their own lives," Gina said. "The wedding is a private affair."

There'll be more bikers than Hollywood people at the wedding.

Zac smiled to himself; he was definitely enjoying his transformation to "biker dude." He didn't dare scan the crowd but he knew their biker friends were there somewhere.

"There you have it folks," the reporter spoke into her microphone as they entered the building. "We *still* have no idea if or when these two will actually tie the knot."

Zac tried to ignore the little voice in his head that wondered the same thing. Gina wore his ring on her finger, and he knew she loved him. But deep inside, he was terrified that this new rush of *Fame* would push her away.

Zac had seriously considered "retiring" from acting. After all, the empty longing that had driven him for so many years was banished, and he knew how Gina felt about it. But to his surprise, Gina disagreed. And he had to admit, she'd been right. He still loved it. And he had some truly rabid fans that wanted to see him on screen again. It had been good for their movie. But would it destroy his chance to make Gina his wife?

They mingled in the lobby area, greeting their backers. Gina had refused both Jed's and Sylvester's offers, opting instead to open the production to crowdfunding. And thanks to the impact of *True Surrender* the campaign had been more than successful. As a result, they weren't beholden to anyone.

They were ushered to their seats and after a few spoken kudos, the lights went down.

He'd thought watching *True Surrender* in this place was emotional. But tonight, with Gina beside him, and considering everything they'd been through…he was more blessed than he deserved to be.

"Zac…" Gina's nails dug into his arm. She had a look of wonder on her face. He knew the feeling.

"What do you think?" He bowed his ear toward her.

"It's…it's…"

When she didn't say anything more, he raised his head to look at her. There were tears in her eyes. "It was all you," she whispered.

"No." He gripped her hand tightly. "It was *us*. Together. We make a great team."

She traced her fingers over the outline of his dialysis graft. Desire tightened in his groin. "I've been thinking," she whispered.

"What about?" he said.

"We'd make a great husband-and-wife team, too."

Everything in his world went stock still. Even the film faded to inconsequence.

"What do you think of a Christmas wedding?" she continued. "It's only four months away…"

"Gina," he breathed. "I would marry you tomorrow or in ten years…whatever it takes. I just want to belong to you. For good."

"I just wanted to know…" she said.

He understood exactly what she meant. "And do you?" he said. "Do you really know beyond a doubt?"

"Oh, yes," she said. "You have the staying power. And you're going to need it as soon as I get you back to the hotel!"

from the author

I hope you enjoyed *Take Two: a Hollywood Romance!* If you'd like to be notified when the next book in The Lady Biker Series is ready, please subscribe to my newsletter or follow me on Facebook or Twitter:

Web site/blog: **www.TraceyCramerKelly.com**

Facebook: **www.Facebook.com/TraceyCramerKelly**

Twitter: **www.Twitter.com/TraceyCramerKel**

MEET THE LADY BIKERS!

The Iron Zebra is a fictional bar (and motorcycle club) that was originally the setting for the "Cool Rider" music video (www. CoolRiderProject.com). It is the preferred hangout of some other fascinating women riders who will soon be telling their stories.

Willow lives her life fast and hard—and she likes her men that way too. Dating only bikers fits her lifestyle—until she literally runs into Mitchell Connor, a local rancher who disdains motorcycles in favor of horses.

When *Andie* returns home to manage the family affairs, she discovers her father was a slum lord. When she becomes the target of unscrupulous tenants, she is forced to turn to the one man her absent U.S. Marine brother swears she can trust: Tor Jorgenson, the object of her fierce crush ten years ago.

Although the man of *Sabrina*'s heart left her twelve years ago to pursue a career in the military, she's done okay for herself running The Iron Zebra. But at 35, she receives a double whammy: a life-altering diagnosis and the return of her lost love (and the father of her son), Captain Chaz Berington.

OTHER TITLES BY TRACEY CRAMER-KELLY

True Surrender

When Major Aaron Bricewick is rescued from Afghanistan terrorists, he thinks the worst is over. But his personal journey is just beginning…

The first surprise is the amputation of his leg. The second is the woman he left behind, now a widow with a 4-year-old son – and his new prosthetist (artificial limb maker). He vows that losing his leg won't derail his career. But maintaining his outward appearance as a got-it-together officer becomes increasingly difficult. And though he has no intention of expanding his life to include a woman, his heart has other ideas – and he finds himself questioning the very foundation of his personal beliefs. When violence – and unexpected redemption – touch his life again, Aaron must make a stand. Which will he choose: duty or love?

Last Chance Rescue

Two search-and-rescue team members must fight their own defenses and let down their walls to rescue each other.

When Brad Sievers runs into his old friend Jessie Van Dyke at his high school reunion, little does he know how much it will change his life. When his high-powered advertising career fizzles, he falls into a most unlikely career opportunity — becoming a member of Jessie's search-and-rescue team. Through dangerous rescues and personal trials, Brad and Jessie become close friends. When Brad is severely injured in a training accident, Jessie nurses him back to health. And when she goes missing one night, Brad realizes just how important she has become to him.

Made in the USA
Charleston, SC
30 September 2013